DAMAGED

JEANNE ST. JAMES

~

Editor: The Twitching Pen
Cover Art: FuriousFotog

~

www.jeannestjames.com

Sign up for my newsletter for insider information, author news, and new releases:
www.jeannestjames.com/newslettersignup

FOREWORD

Please note: This book was previously published under the title *Banged Up*. It has been reedited and republished for your enjoyment!

CHAPTER 1

As Mace Walker slid the key into the lock, an immediate sense of relief washed over him. He hadn't been home in…*Hell*, forever. Even though he owned the house and considered it his home, he felt like a stranger when he opened the front door. He chucked his keys on the table by the door with a sigh. He'd been home for a whole thirty seconds and restlessness already ate at him.

The house was quiet, and he wondered where his sister was. Probably sleeping, *dummy*, since it was—he glanced at his watch—freaking one in the morning. Most normal folk slept at this hour. But then, he wasn't normal. He couldn't be to do his job.

But, he couldn't do his job right now, anyway. He'd been forced home to heal. Against his wishes.

Fucking bullshit.

The foyer was dark, but he didn't need to hit the light. He still knew the house well enough. He made his way to the stairs where he dumped his duffle bags on the floor and ran a hand through his too-long hair.

Those two small duffels held little evidence of his life for the past couple years—just some toiletries and a few basic items of clothing.

He turned toward the kitchen, and the foyer lit up, blinding him

1

for a second. He blinked against the harsh light, and a young voice rang out from the top of the steps. "Hold it right there! Put your arms up and back away from the stairs."

What the fuck?

Mace had expected to see his sister bounding down the stairway of his two-story colonial, excited after not seeing him for the past two years. Actually, more like one year, eleven months, and fifteen days. Not that he'd counted.

But instead, he stared up into the deadly eye of a Glock. And from his viewpoint, it looked like a model 27, a .40 caliber—a compact, but still a decent sized gun in a very small, very uneasy hand. Instantly, the hairs on the back of his neck rose.

Damn.

He'd dealt with crime bosses and their flunkies—from drug to porno rings—and had managed to survive. Now he was going to be killed by some measly punk he surprised while burglarizing his house when he happened to come home? The cruel irony made him want to laugh. Instead, he did as instructed. With caution, he raised his hands above his head before stepping back toward the middle of the foyer. He avoided standing directly under the light, trying to get a better view of the top of the steps. But he didn't have much success; the upstairs hallway and the upper section of the stairway were hidden in shadows.

If he played his cards right, this little situation would be under his control in no time at all. He just had to keep the kid calm and make the skinny punk believe he was the one in command. The Glock didn't have a conventional safety. All the kid had to do was pull the trigger and pull it again and again until all the rounds in the clip emptied into Mace's body. And from what he could see in the limited light, the kid's fingers twitched from nervousness.

Not a good sign.

Where had a young punk gotten an expensive handgun like that? It certainly hadn't been in the house. And if it had been, it would have been locked up in the gun safe.

If only he could see the boy's face. He needed to see the eyes. Without seeing those, Mace couldn't even begin to predict what the kid would do.

"Don't you dare move, or I'll blow your face off!" The kid's voice raised an octave, making him sound more and more like…a female.

Mace tensed when the person started down the steps. At first, he could see bare toes, a slim calf, then another. His gaze flicked to the gun before returning to the shapely naked thighs which couldn't belong to a kid. No fucking way. Especially not a boy. Those smooth legs definitely belonged to a woman, and he couldn't wait to see the rest of her.

So far, the view almost made it worth being held at gunpoint. Almost.

He felt strangely disappointed when an oversized T-shirt—*shit, was that Sponge Bob on it?*—blocked his view of creamy flesh. His arms were tired, his leg throbbed painfully, and his patience was wearing thin. But he still wouldn't move since he had no idea who this woman descending the stairs was. His curiosity piqued when she stepped down into the light, which highlighted her long, curly red hair and made her wide, *glaring* green eyes sparkle and snap.

Lightning shot through him and landed in his groin. Neither fear nor pain made him suck in his breath. No, her unencumbered breasts bobbing under the cotton shirt with each step she took did. Her nipples stood out like two beacons under the worn cotton.

Jesus.

He had to clear his throat twice before he could ask her, "You're robbing this house dressed like that?"

Really, if it wasn't for the gun being pointed at him center mass, he wouldn't be taking this seriously at all.

When she hesitated halfway down the staircase, a look of uncertainty crossed her features, before disappearing as quickly as it came. Her eyes narrowed, and she scowled at him. "Am I robbing this house? The question is: What are you doing here?"

His leg began to throb again, the way it had earlier on his long drive into town. Although, he preferred the ache to no feeling at all. He was glad to even still have his leg. Hell, he was lucky just to be alive.

Well, alive at the moment. It wouldn't take much to change that.

"I live here."

She frowned, her eyebrows knitting together. No surprise that she didn't believe him.

"Can I put my arms down now?" His fists clenched high above his head, and he fought not only the pain, but also the urge to drop them to rub his thigh.

"No! Don't move! I'm going to call the cops. Back up." She jabbed the gun in his direction.

He didn't move. Instead, he released a long, very loud, impatient sigh.

"Back up, I said! Or I'll shoot you."

"It's happened before," he said dryly.

The redhead looked at him in surprise, her feet faltering on the last step. "What?"

"I've been shot before. So go ahead. Apparently, I have nine lives." He tried not to smirk. Irritating a woman with a gun wasn't smart. Experience, and he had plenty of it, had taught him that much.

Adjusting her grip on the gun, her knuckles turned even whiter. "Well, your luck has run out, asshole."

Asshole? Damn. Harsh. He hadn't done anything yet to be insulted like that. "What's in your clip?" She glanced at the gun with just a quick flick of her eyes, but he caught it. "Ever shoot someone? Ever *seen* someone shot? Besides on TV or in a movie, of course. It's pretty fucking messy."

The arm holding the black, lightweight gun trembled.

"Did you ever hear of the saying, 'Don't pull it, unless you're going to use it?' If you decide to use it, make sure you use both hands. Be sure you kill me, not maim me." He patted his palm on his chest. "Two shots. Right here. Center mass. If you're going to do it, do it right."

4

"*Shut up!*"

He did.

The woman placed her free hand underneath the butt of the gun to support it. At least she seemed open to suggestions. However, his talking had unnerved her, and he didn't need her to squeeze the trigger by accident. No matter what type of ammo she had in that clip, all bullets tend to hurt. He frowned.

"Lie on the floor! Your hands behind your head! Now!"

Christ, the bitch was getting annoying now. But at this point, she was close enough to kill him, even with a bad shot. He had enough with the games for tonight. Exhausted, he just wanted to go to sleep in his own bed in his own house.

Mace judged the distance. "Can't." He only needed her a few steps closer. She waved the gun at him recklessly, her left foot moving forward. "Do it!"

One more step…

"I can't kneel easily. I've got a bum leg." The bum leg was true enough, but he exaggerated a bit on the kneeling part. He'd been known to lie when he had a gun directed at him. Sometimes lies came easier than truths. And he'd had a lot of practice at that, too.

"From all those times being shot, huh?"

"Actually, yeah."

"Down on the ground, or I'll blow your brains all over the foyer." Her slow words, muttered through gritted teeth, made him think she might be serious. Her right foot moved to keep her balance.

Now was his chance.

Mace lunged. He cracked her extended arm with his fist, causing a sharp cry of pain from her. The gun dropped, skittered across the tile floor, and she grabbed her injured wrist. He grasped both her flailing arms by the wrists and pushed her backward. When she fell back onto the stairs, air whooshed from her lungs, and her head missed the edge of a step by a fraction of an inch. He planted his knees on the outside of her bare thighs, pinning them together.

Mace stared down at the woman trapped beneath him. His

weight crushed her into the carpeted steps. And he didn't care. He was in pain, so why shouldn't she be?

"Oh, God, please. Don't—" she whispered, her voice catching. Eyes wide, she sank her teeth into her bottom lip.

He scowled. "Don't what? Hurt you? After you just had a gun pointed at my head, you don't want me to hurt you?"

The pulse in her delicate neck pounded like it wanted to escape.

"If...if you leave now, I won't call the police. I'll forget this ever happened."

Liar. If she got the chance, she'd grab the nearest phone and dial 911.

Mace had no sympathy for her discomfort since he felt a little of his own. Damn, not just a little but a lot. His leg muscle burned like hell. "If you call the police, the only person they'll take away is you."

She twisted underneath him, making him wince in pain. He gritted his teeth to avoid groaning out loud. That groan would not have been a pleasurable one. Not at all. And what a pity. It had been a while since he'd been with a beautiful female like the one beneath him. He'd have to do something about that and soon.

But right now, he had a problem to deal with, and that problem continued to squirm. He didn't feel at all charitable, but he would to have to let her up. For his own sake.

Mace stood, lifting her with him, careful not to release her wrists. He angled away from her slightly, making sure a knee or foot didn't connect with any of his vital areas. He was in enough pain already.

"Who are you, and what are you doing here?"

"I could ask you the same." She exhaled loudly, visibly regaining control of herself.

With a shake of his head, he tightened his grip on her wrists—a little reminder of the change of power. "No. I'm in charge now. Unless you want me to have you dragged out of here cuffed, you'd better answer my fucking questions."

"I'm not going to tell you, a...a *criminal* who I am."

If the situation wasn't so serious, he'd laugh. "I'm not a criminal."

She eyed him skeptically through the long mane of red hair falling over her face. "Okay, so who are you, then?"

Mace let another impatient sigh escape. Maybe he should close his eyes and count to ten...*Nah, fuck it.* "I told you, I live here. And stop trying to screw with me. Just answer my questions."

"I'm not screwing with you. Go ahead and call the police." She flattened her lips together and tilted her chin toward the ceiling.

Christ, she was stubborn. Was he going to have to try another tactic to get her to talk? He was trying to be reasonable, but his options were limited. He really didn't want the local police involved. Not if he could avoid it, anyway. And it wasn't necessary; if he couldn't handle one skinny-assed woman by himself, he needed to give up his day job.

Hell, that wasn't fair, she probably wasn't skinny-assed. She probably had a nice rear on her, one which matched the *very* nice front. He wouldn't mind checking it out, just to make sure. He loved a woman who was nicely balanced—tits and ass.

"If you don't tell me who you are and what you're doing here, I'll strip off this skimpy shirt of yours and anything else you're wearing —which probably isn't much." He raked another look down her long, supple, hot little body. *Fuck.* It had been too long. His cock was already at half-mast just imaging her naked.

The threat was empty, but what little color she had drained away from her face.

Her lower lip trembled, and her eyes widened. "So, you're going to rape me?"

Oh fuck. No. Nonononononono!

Hell no, he wasn't. But he might let the threat idle there between them if it would get her to talk. It made him feel like a complete shit for not clearing up her misconception, though.

And when he remained silent, so did she.

He couldn't believe it; she actually wasn't going to talk. He grasped both her wrists in one hand, and with the other, began to slowly pull up the hem of her nightshirt, revealing pink panties. *Hot damn.* His dick stood at complete attention now, and unfortunately caught in an uncomfortable position. But there was no way he would adjust himself and prove what a horny shit he was.

Before he could raise the soft cotton shirt above her belly —*Goddamn, she was an innie*—she jerked her hips away from him, the color returning to her face in full force.

"Okay, okay! My name is Colby Parks." In what looked like defeat, she closed her eyes.

With a sigh, Mace reluctantly released the shirt, pushed away the slight regret, and watched the fabric catch on her hip. For half a second, he wished she would have been more stubborn, since she obviously wasn't wearing a bra. He would have liked to see what was under the goofy cartoon character. He gave himself a mental shake.

"Colby Parks? Is that your real name?"

"Yes," she whispered and tossed her head, flipping the hair away from her face.

A dusting of freckles crossed her nose. He knew better than to be distracted by something so simple like freckles. But he couldn't help wondering where else she had them. Okay, he needed to concentrate. This woman had pulled a gun on him. In his profession, he couldn't afford to lose his focus. "It must be. Who could make up a name like that? What are you doing here?"

"Housesitting."

"Yeah, right." Mace chuckled. "And doing a bang-up job at it." His humor quickly vanished to deadly seriousness. He pushed his face close to hers. His attempt to intimidate her once again failed when her soft breath, coming quickly through those full, parted lips, sidetracked him. For a second. Or two. "Who hired you?"

Colby Parks' green eyes shot daggers at him. Now he knew where the saying "if looks could kill" came from.

"If you truly live here, you should know that!"

He squeezed her wrists tighter. His eyes narrowed as he muttered, "Lady, I'm not here to play games. Answer the damn question."

She hesitated a second before Mace watched the resignation cross her face. Damn, he was a little disappointed she gave up so easily. He liked her fire…more than liked it.

"Maxi…Maxine Walker."

Ah, so that's why his sister didn't greet him. She was out of town and hired this little gun-toting vixen to watch the house.

Mace released her without warning, and Colby stumbled away, rubbing her wrists, then turned and sprinted into the kitchen. He followed right behind her, making sure he stayed between her and the gun. Of course, she did exactly what he expected. He depressed the hook switch on the phone while she frantically dialed. While he held it down, he did a quick assessment for any nearby cell phones. He doubted she was packing one in her panties.

"Don't bother calling the police. It might not turn out well for you."

Colby held the handset to her chest like a lifeline. She stared at him, wide-eyed. The pressure of the handset against the thin, worn cotton only emphasized what he struggled not to notice and didn't want to admit to noticing in the first place. He turned away, picked up the gun, stuffed it into his jacket pocket, and limped to the kitchen table.

With a groan, he slowly sank into a hard, wooden chair and dragged a hand through his hair. "I'm Mace Walker. Maxi's brother." He didn't bother to look at her. He hoped she would make the right choice at this point.

The receiver clattered onto its base behind him. Huh, he was right. Imagine that. He massaged his right thigh, gritting his teeth against the pain.

"Maxi's brother." The whisper also came from behind him, but within another second, she stood in front of him, hands jammed on her hips, eyes narrowed. "She doesn't have a brother."

Mace looked at the gathered cotton at her waist, trying to ignore —though failing miserably—the way the hem of the shirt now sat cockeyed, almost flashing those pink panties. Those panties probably smelled so sweet. He massaged his thigh harder.

"Well, if she doesn't, then I'm just a figment of your imagination." She shot him an incredulous look. "I've known Maxi for over a year, and she has never—not once—mentioned a brother. And she certainly didn't tell me he'd be visiting."

She remained frozen for a minute and appeared undecided about how to proceed. With an exasperated huff, she pulled out the chair across from him. And with a tug on the hem of her nightshirt, she settled into it. The tug, a sad attempt at covering her long length of thigh, covered that sweet little package wrapped in pink satin.

Okay, concentrate, damn it.

"She doesn't tell anyone she has a brother, so no one asks questions." He stood and left the kitchen, returning a few moments later with a prescription bottle. Making sure she was paying attention, he pulled the gun out of his pocket, released the full clip and unloaded the round in the chamber. A chill ran up his spine when the lone hollow-point bullet rolled across the kitchen table. *She really could have shot him.* He tossed the empty gun in her lap, making her jump. Leave it to a woman to be more dangerous than the Mafia. *Fuck.*

"I hope you have a license for that." Mace stuck the clip in his jacket pocket and went to the cabinet for a glass.

Relief flooded him when he found the glasses in the same cabinet after almost two years. He had horrible visions of his sister taking over his house and redecorating it all girly-like. Luckily, she had enough sense to leave things be.

When he crossed to the sink, he realized he was wrong. Maxi changed something. He frowned at the little yellow ceramic duck with a blue ribbon tied around its neck which held a sponge. That would have to go.

After filling the glass with cold tap water, he swallowed a pill and took a drink. On second thought, he popped another. He settled across from Colby again, studying her while he waited for the painkillers to kick in. Her mouth pressed into a tight line—a shame for those luscious lips—and he could see the wheels turning in her head.

"Why wouldn't she want anyone to know she has a brother? Were you in jail?" Her eyebrows rose. "Are you an escaped convict?"

Mace shook his head and couldn't help but smile. She had to be kidding. "Yeah, I'm an escaped convict, and you're my hostage. You must do what I say. Get naked and lie on the table."

Mace watched for a reaction. Nothing. He was losing his touch.

Colby looked stone-cold, not even a twitch of a smile. "I want to see some proof of who you say you are."

Lady, someone must have burned you good to make you so mistrustful you have to interrogate a friend's brother. Oh, and carry a gun. He couldn't forget that. But, honestly, he didn't blame her. He would be just as cautious and suspicious if he were in her shoes—he glanced down at her naked feet—or in those cute, pink painted toes.

"What, knowing where the drinking glasses are kept isn't proof enough?"

"Don't toy with me. I want to see some ID."

Her determination fascinated him. So did everything else about her. It's not every day he came across a woman like her—strong-minded, not afraid of guns, and one hell of a hottie...a redheaded, green-eyed, freckled one to boot. Colby reminded him of an uptight school teacher—the kind who would let her hair down and get wild at night.

She might be a sex kitten under her stubborn exterior. His type of woman. Mace grinned. His mind drifted back to their conversation, and he realized she was waiting for his answer. "ID? Like my inmate's ID card with my mug shot and number on it?"

"Any ID would do."

"Sorry, I left it behind when I scaled the walls. Had to pack light. It was a long swim from Alcatraz to land." Unfortunately, she didn't seem to appreciate his dry sense of humor. The pain in his leg slowly eased, and he released a contented sigh. But his relief was short-lived

11

since, for some reason, he now had a headache. He glanced over at the reason. "Where is my dear sister, anyhow?"

"Away."

"Yeah, thanks for that. I realize she wouldn't have needed a housesitter if she was only on a date."

"She's on her honeymoon."

Mace straightened up, his eyes narrowing. "Honeymoon?" He tried to read her expression, but it was nonexistent. At the moment, she was a rock.

"Yes, you know, the trip you go on after you get married?"

He ignored the dig, thinking her humor no better than his. "She got married? To who? When? Where did she go?"

Colby leaned back in her chair and crossed her arms over her chest. Mace wanted to protest because he could no longer see the hard pebbles of her nipples through her shirt.

"If you're her brother, why don't you know that information? Why weren't you at the wedding? Did you have a falling out, or were you really in prison?"

"Neither. We were separated by necessity." The half-assed explanation sounded lame, even to his own ears.

"Separated by necessity," she said slowly, the words rolling around in her mouth like she could taste them. "And how long was this so-called separation?"

"I don't know." Of course, he knew. But saying it out loud made it sound worse. "Two years," he mumbled.

"Two years," she repeated with a frown. "Then, you'll just have to wait until she gets back. I don't feel I should tell you her personal business if she didn't tell you herself."

With a weary sigh, Mace rubbed a hand over his eyes. Too tired to argue, he said, "And when will that be?"

"In two months."

Mace cursed softly. Two months? Who goes on a honeymoon for two months? "I might not be here that long."

"You won't be here at all. I wasn't given any instructions about letting visitors stay while she was away. So, you'll just have to hide out somewhere else."

He cocked an eyebrow in surprise. *Fuck. That.* "Hate to tell you, but I own this house."

He grinned when Colby stiffened in her chair, and her hands landed back in her lap.

COLBY PUSHED to her feet and laid the gun on the table, studying the man across from her. Mace Walker's presence alone had been enough to rattle her at first, but now, conflicting emotions tore her in two different directions. He said he was Maxi's brother. This house was his, not hers. Why hadn't Maxi told her? Could she trust him? He certainly didn't look trustworthy.

His intensely dark, almost black eyes and his unshaven face unnerved her. His dark clothes seemed suspicious, and his oversized, bulky leather jacket was large enough to conceal something. Creeping into the house after dark made him even more suspect. Maybe she should call the police anyway. Though, he did sort of look like Maxi, but in a more beefy, masculine way.

"I still want to see some ID," she repeated, more firmly this time.

With a grumble, he pulled out his wallet and flipped it open. A photo ID was tucked in the clear plastic front pocket, but he didn't remove it, and she couldn't see it clearly from where she stood. Instead, he dug until he found something specific.

He handed her an old, expired driver's license, one in which he looked much younger...and his expression looked worry-free. No frown lines marred the man looking at her from the photo, but it proved he was Macen Jeffrey Walker, and the address listed this house.

"What, you haven't had a driver's license since you were..." Colby glanced at the date. "Eighteen? Been in the slammer that long?" She did some quick figuring on his age. Thirty-six. Even though she now had serious doubts he'd ever been imprisoned, she wanted to pay him back for scaring her earlier. It was only fair.

"No. Not any with my real name on them."

"Ah. So what do you do, Mr. Walker, that you haven't seen or even talked to your sister in two years, don't have a current driver's license with your own name on it, and have to creep into your own house after dark?" She flipped the license back to him. She couldn't wait to hear his explanation. And she really wanted to see the more current ID he refused to pull out of his wallet. What did he hide?

He caught the license in midair and took his time tucking it back into his wallet before answering her. "Oh, this and that. You know, a lot of traveling."

"No, I don't know."

"That's too bad, Colby."

She wasn't sure what he meant. But one thing she was sure about was her name on his lips bothered her, for more reasons than she wanted to admit. "Not really. Your job wouldn't have anything to do with manufacturing license plates, would it?"

"Sort of. I do the hiring, in a way." He stiffly pushed himself up from the chair and swept long fingers through his coffee-colored hair, the kind of coffee he probably drank. Black and strong. "Well, I'm beat. I'm going up to bed."

"Wait…" She followed him into the foyer and saw two bags sitting by the staircase. She hadn't noticed them earlier in the tussle. "I still don't think this is a good idea."

As he leaned down to pick up his duffel bags, his hand gripped the banister tightly, so tightly she wouldn't be surprised if there were indentations from his fingers in the wood.

"Honestly, I don't care what you think. I'm tired. This is my house. And I'm going to my bed. Those are the facts. Live with them or leave."

He clearly struggled to keep a blank face. Simply climbing up the steps caused white brackets around his pressed lips.

But he couldn't just walk away leaving it like this. Should she stay? Should she go? And if he wanted her to go, should she leave now or in the morning? Colby followed him up the steps. She decided to test him. "If it's okay, I'll gather my things in the morning."

Mace stopped abruptly at the top of the stairway before turning to tower over her. She halted in her tracks, instinctively grabbing the banister for balance.

"You don't have to leave. Since Maxi hired you, you can stay and finish your job. I don't know how long I'll be in town, anyway. I'd hate to have to find another housesitter on a moment's notice when we have a perfectly good one already."

Colby wanted to collapse in relief. She had nowhere else to go; the house she was renovating wouldn't be habitable for at least another two months. That's why she was so grateful to Maxi for letting her house sit. The timing had been perfect...well, except for this little snag.

Little wasn't the word for him. He had to be six foot three with his boots on. She was sure his jacket made him look heavier than he really was. But his legs were long and lean, especially encased in those sinfully snug, worn blue jeans. Damn, but she could appreciate a man with a good ass in well-fitted jeans.

Mace suddenly turned away to continue down the hall. Maybe he didn't like women staring at him. Still, it was only fair after his eyes burned her bare skin earlier.

She trailed him to the end of the hall, keeping her distance when he pulled out a ring of keys and inserted one into the first door on the left. She had wondered why the room across from hers was locked and even attempted to open it one day while she vacuumed. Maxi's room was down the hall, and Colby slept in one of the guest rooms.

Now it made sense...the secret room of the secret brother.

She tried to peer around him when he swung open the door but only saw the dust rising behind him when he flipped on the light.

She wanted to follow him in to see the locked sanctuary, but he blocked her view and her way when he turned to face her.

"Well, good night."

Colby extended a hand to stop the door from slamming in her face. She showed him her empty gun. "What about my clip?"

Mace frowned. "You'll get it back when you show me you know how to properly handle and shoot the thing. Go to bed." And with that, he slammed the door shut.

Colby stood, one fist planted on her hip, staring at the closed door for a few minutes. She listened to the muffled rustling and wondered what he was doing. *Getting ready for bed, most likely, genius.*

Tomorrow would be soon enough for her to dig for more information on him. Right now, she would take his advice and go to bed.

Back in her room, she placed the gun on the nightstand so it would be within arm's reach. He might have handed her back an empty gun but...

She smiled as she opened the nightstand drawer. Inside it lay another clip. Along with two more boxes of ammo.

MACE THREW his bags on the bed and sank down beside them. He ran a hand through his already tousled hair while letting out a long, soothing sigh. He surveyed the master bedroom. A layer of dust coated the furniture, a few framed pictures of his late parents and his sister sat around the room, and his alarm clock had never been reset after the last power outage. It flashed 12:00 incessantly. He glanced at his watch. Almost two-thirty now. Damn.

But he was home. *Really home.* Not in some strange motel in some unknown town surrounded by people who shouldn't be classified as human.

He was sick of the city life: the noise, the rush, and the constant wariness. A lot of the tension in his body dissipated the moment he drove into Malvern. It was different, more laid back, and even as a large college town, its population was only a fraction of New York City's.

He was disappointed, though. He had looked forward to spending time with his sister, the only person who really understood him. Someone who he could be completely honest with.

He wanted to run things by her, bend her ear a bit. Hell, more like a lot. He needed to figure out his future. But now, he'd have to wait— wait to be around someone who loved him for who he really was.

Not loved or even hated him for who he pretended to be.

He didn't know how long he would last, doing what he did. The job had taken a toll. Spending time with people he reviled and couldn't trust exhausted him. He was tired of having to agonizingly memorize details of a made-up life, an existence where one slip-up could cost his life or a colleague's.

He rubbed his thigh. His last assignment had been a killer, both emotionally and physically. He just needed time now.

Time to forget.

Time to heal.

He thought about the redhead just across the hall from him. He felt a twinge of guilt about his brusqueness toward her. On the other hand, it was hard to be nice when you're being threatened with a loaded weapon. Though, admittedly, she impressed him with her guts and determination, whether it was real or just an act to cover her fear.

Mace anticipated his time home would be boring. Dull. Uneventful. Colby Parks just might have changed that.

CHAPTER 2

C OLBY STIRRED the eggs around the frying pan, scrambling them. She was exhausted since she hardly slept last night, too busy listening to every creak in the dark. Each time she thought she heard footsteps, she'd sat straight up in bed, reaching for her gun. It ended up being nothing, and this morning, she felt like an idiot. A huge one.

Being it was Saturday, her usual plan to go over to the house to check on the status of the renovations was the only thing on her schedule.

Since she was sinking her life savings into the old house, she needed to make sure everything was going smoothly. Plus, she wanted to finish painting the kitchen.

The cabinets were done, but the walls were only spackled and primed, ready to complete. She hoped the yellow color she picked would help cheer up the dreary room. She wasn't sure. The only thing she was sure of was she stunk at interior decorating. But she just couldn't afford to hire—

"Mmm. Smells good. Got enough for one more?"

The spatula clattered into the pan, flinging bits of egg onto the stovetop. She took two deep breaths to try to slow her heart rate before retrieving the utensil and turning to face the intruder.

The reason why she hadn't gotten more than a few winks of sleep last night entered the small kitchen, pushing his slightly damp hair away from his face. He wore an old, threadbare black T-shirt and black sweatpants. Since when did ratty sweatpants ever look sexy on a man? And he was barefoot, his long toes wiggling against the cool linoleum floor.

"Sure."

He looked at home grabbing the freshly squeezed grapefruit juice she had set on the table earlier and pouring himself a glass. Well, he should, she guessed, since it really was his home. Whether she liked it or not.

"Sleep well?"

"Of course," she lied. She hid a chuckle with her hand when he made a disgusted face after the first swallow. The juice tasted a little bitter, and she preferred it that way. It was one reason why she squeezed it herself.

Mace wiped his mouth with the back of his wrist. "Jeez, any coffee?"

Colby shook her head. "Don't drink it."

He cocked an eyebrow at her. "Yeah? What sane person doesn't like coffee?" He moved around the kitchen, opening cabinets until he found an old, stained coffee maker. He dragged it out, cleared some counter space, and plugged it in.

"I try to eat healthy," she explained.

She couldn't help but notice he himself looked quite healthy this morning. And, in the light of day, very edible. The cotton tee clung to his broad shoulders and the curves of his chest, accentuating his chiseled pecs. He hunted through the drawers, every little movement causing his biceps to flex against the snug sleeves of his shirt. He was built, but lean, not like an overly huge, ripped body builder. Those details hadn't been visible last night when he wore that bulky jacket. She turned her attention back to the pan before he caught her drooling.

Mace dug up some filters from a drawer and then went to the

refrigerator. He let out a low curse and slammed the freezer door. "No coffee! You'd at least think my sister would have left some." Suddenly, he was behind her, peering over her shoulder into the frying pan. "I thought eggs were bad for you."

The scent of fresh soap wafting over her, combined with his close body heat, caused her pulse to quicken. Despite not shaving his face this morning, in the light of day, he looked much less like the criminal she thought he was last night.

Unless it was a crime to look that good.

"Only if you eat them a lot. A couple a week won't kill you. They're good protein." She removed a loaf of multi-grain bread from the breadbox.

"That's good to know. I think I'm more worried about the gun you have killing me than a couple of artery-clogging eggs."

A chair scraped the floor behind her.

"I slept well too, by the way. It was nice to be in my own bed," he said.

"Yeah, I bet those prison cots aren't too comfortable."

She heard a half-assed groan. "Again? When are you going to stop with the prison cracks?"

Colby shrugged and bit back a smile, popping four slices of bread into the toaster. "When I run out of them."

She schooled the humor from her face before turning. He studied her from where he sat at the table—most likely wondering why she was dressed like a construction worker. She wore her denim overalls over a plain white T-shirt with the oversized short sleeves rolled up. The clunky, steel-toed boots she had on weren't very feminine either. Definitely not a sexy look for her, but you wouldn't know it from his heated gaze.

"Are you a construction worker?"

"Sort of," she replied, echoing his equivocation from last night. She plopped a tub of Irish butter on the table.

"It's a sin to keep that hair of yours pulled back."

She was close enough for him to tug on her long, heavy braid.

21

The sight of his large hand sliding along her hair made her breath catch. And it wasn't from fear. That was the scary part.

She yanked her head, releasing her hair from his grasp, and stepped back, giving herself a cushion of safety. "Well, I have to tie it back to keep it out of paint and plaster." She pointed the spatula at his hair. "Speaking of sin…It's a sin for a man to have such long, full hair like yours. I bet some women are envious. Men, too."

He dragged a hand through it. "It needs a cut," he admitted ruefully.

Colby didn't think so. It seemed to fit him. Not that she knew much about him. She wondered again why he had kept out of his sister's life for two years. When she couldn't sleep last night, her head had filled with too many questions. A strange man sleeping just across the hallway didn't help either. Yes, the lack of sleep could be attributed to her being cautious around a stranger, not because he disturbed her in other ways—ways she didn't want to admit.

Mace cut into her thoughts. "What are you painting and plastering?"

"A house," she said absently, scooping eggs onto two plates and then adding the toast. She slid a plate in front of him. "Don't bother to ask for bacon."

"I wouldn't dream of it." He speared the eggs with his fork. "Whose house? Is that what you do for a living?"

Colby rolled her eyes. "No way. It's a dirty job." She sat down and grabbed a small container from the center of the table. A swig of grapefruit juice helped her down a couple of vitamin supplements. She offered him the bottle. "Want some?"

Mace shook his head and pulled out his own bottle from his pocket—the same bottle from last night. He popped two white, oblong pills. "I have my own."

"What are they?" Colby looked at the prescription curiously. Before she could read the label, he tucked it back in his pocket.

"Strong vitamins."

Colby lifted an eyebrow at him but refrained from commenting. His business, his problem.

"So, whose house are you getting dirty over?"

She swallowed a mouthful of eggs. "Mine. I bought an old house. I'm fixing it up."

"By yourself?" He looked intrigued.

She shook her head. "No. During the week, I have a contractor doing most of the work. On the weekends, I like to go out there and dawdle around. Do little things here and there. Most of the time, I end up sitting in the middle of a half-finished room, daydreaming about what it will look like when the project's completed."

Mace polished off his breakfast and then eyed the lone piece of toast remaining on Colby's plate. "Sounds like quite a task."

She offered the piece to him. He accepted, sinking his white teeth into the crispy toast while she still held it, barely grazing the tip of her finger. He grinned when she jerked her hand away.

The only way she refrained from trembling was by curling her fingers into a fist while trying to keep on the subject at hand. She didn't want him to know how he affected her. "It is. It's all I've got. All my money—all the money I've earned—is in that house. I can't wait until it's finished."

Taking the empty plates over to the sink to wash them gave her an excuse to distance herself from him, but he followed right behind. He grabbed the dish towel before she could.

So much for creating a little distance, since he stood close to take the wet dishes from her to help dry. And each time she handed him one, he would brush his fingers against hers. This did not help her nerves.

"Wouldn't it be easier to build from scratch?"

"Maybe. But that's not the point. The house needed saving. I felt it in my bones the first time I saw it. I don't think it's right to tear down an old building just because it needs a little work. The house has history since many lives have gone through it. If only walls could talk."

"Maybe it's better they can't. Otherwise, I'd be blackmailed by many, many walls by now."

Colby leaned her hip against the counter, drying her hands. She considered his strong, angular jaw covered by light olive skin and dark stubble. "Ah, so you *have* done many bad things in your life, huh, Macen Walker?"

"Just call me Mace. To answer your question: not necessarily. I just wouldn't want all my shit out there. Good or bad. It's my story to tell."

"Like why you've kept away from your sister for so long?"

"There was a good reason for that, and I'd rather not talk about it." He folded the dish towel with great care, placed it on the counter, and turned to face her. "Instead, I'd like to come along with you and see this house of yours which needs so much work."

His offer was the last thing she expected. He stepped a little closer, and for a moment, she thought he may grab her. Under normal circumstances, his proximity would be too close for her comfort; strange men made her uneasy. But this one…This one did something else to her—awoke some feelings she almost forgot about.

Colby shook herself mentally. What was she thinking? She'd just met the guy, and all she could think about was how good-looking and mysterious he was, all wrapped up in a sexy package. Just looking at him caused her lower body to react. Her panties dampened, and her nipples pebbled almost painfully. This was not like her. Not at all.

But he was Maxi's brother. She trusted Maxi. And so far this morning, this man had been nothing but kind and, mostly, non-threatening. At this point, she had no reason not to trust him. Well, except for the little issue of where he had disappeared to for the last two years. There was that. Which was a little weird.

It had been a while since she'd been alone with someone like him. A man who was all male, one who made her think of sex and not fear. And this morning, sex was all she could think about when she looked at Mace.

She opened her mouth to turn him down, but instead, she said, "Great, but we'll have to take your car." She assumed he had one though she hadn't bothered to look. "I

planned on riding my bike over."

His eyebrows shot up, and he looked like he was about to question her but suddenly changed his mind. "No problem. We'll take my truck." He gave her a quick smile. "I'll go get ready."

Colby watched him leave the kitchen to change. The last thing she expected was for a mysterious man to come walking into her life. And she should be afraid, very afraid. Suddenly, her quiet little life, one she had worked very hard for, was going to get flipped upside down. She wasn't sure she was ready for it.

And if he thought he would remain mysterious, he was wrong. Dead wrong.

MACE PARKED his F-150 extended cab in front of the huge, looming old house. It took all his strength to close his dropped jaw. Overgrown, weedy rose bushes surrounded the monstrosity. The lawn appeared barren in some spots and overgrown in others. He tried not to cringe when he saw it, but Colby caught him.

"Oh, it won't be so bad after a fresh coat of paint and the wrap-around porch is repaired. I have a landscaper coming in a couple of weeks to take care of the yard."

Mace didn't have the heart to tell her it needed more than that. Way more. The old copper gutters—blackish-green from weathering —hung away from the eaves in places, some of the shutters were MIA and the rest...the rest should be just torn down. Hell, he could see the porch roof sagging from where he sat.

"You have to see the inside to really appreciate it." She jumped out of the truck, and he followed reluctantly.

"I'm sure," he murmured.

He really doubted it. What he didn't doubt was how she felt about the place. Colby's face lit up when they walked through the wrought iron gate. Beauty *was* in the eye of the beholder. And that eye wasn't in his head. He thought the house looked like it was the set of a horror movie—a "B" movie at best.

The only beauty on this property was the slender redhead walking in front of him. He found himself mesmerized by the rock-n-roll of her hips. Even in those god-awful denim overalls, she was fuckable. His cock got hard just thinking about it. Sliding into her tight, wet—

"Careful." She took his elbow when they reached the porch and guided him cautiously, apparently knowing just where to step to avoid the rotting floorboards.

Good thing she showed him the way because her luscious lips sorely distracted him. When she ran her tongue across them, he bit back a groan. Damn, he was no better than a horny teenager. But he couldn't deny he wanted those lips on a certain hard part of his anatomy. Hell, anywhere on his body would work.

When they got to the entryway, Colby stopped short, the smile on her face widening. Mace closed his eyes for a second, willing himself to behave. When he opened them again, the first thing he saw was the front double doors needed a good scraping and a fresh coat of paint. Even so, Colby ran her fingers lovingly over one of the oval, stained glass panels. His cock jerked with every slide of her fingers. He desperately wanted to reach down and adjust himself. But he fought it. *Hard.*

"Just look at these. I can't walk into this house without stopping to admire these beautiful doors. I had the stained glass replaced in them. When I bought the place, almost all the windows in the house were broken."

Once he could think straight, Mace had to admit the doors were pretty nice. But he couldn't base his opinion on the house by the front doors alone; he was now curious about the inside. It couldn't be worse and not be boarded up, even condemned.

"How long have you owned it?"

"The bank and I have owned it for five months."

"I'm surprised the bank would mortgage a project like this."

Colby turned to him in surprise. "Why?"

Ah fuck. Foot meet mouth. "Uh, because it..." *Because it was a dump, and no loan officer in his right mind would—*"Because insurance. I bet it was difficult to insure something this old."

"Nope. No problem." She unlocked the door and stepped inside.

Good. She had insurance on it. The best thing would be to burn the place down and start from scratch. *If only insurance fraud wasn't a federal offense.* He shook his head, following her over the threshold.

Later, Mace had to admit the place had character and understood why Colby loved it so much. She was doing a good job restoring it with the help of the contractors. But obviously, it would be a long, slow process.

They sat on the floor in the empty, oversized dining room. Their "picnic" lunch was spread out on a drop cloth in the center of a wood floor in desperate need of refinishing. Colby had packed leftover fried chicken and some homemade potato salad.

From the two meals she fed him so far, she seemed a decent cook. He could get used to eating like this very easily. Eating by himself in greasy dumps or fast food restaurants had gotten old quickly. They ate in companionable silence until they were both full. But he wasn't fully sated...yet.

With a food-induced contented sigh, Mace stared up at the intricate woodwork bordering the ceiling and the walls. At least the stained wainscoting, which lined the walls below a chair rail, appeared in decent shape and didn't need a coat of paint. "This house is pretty large for one person."

"Yep. But I love big houses. And I don't mind living alone. I'm quite capable of taking care of myself now."

Although it caught his attention, he let the "now" part go for the moment. "I've noticed," he answered instead, thinking about the gun she had stashed in her purse. She brought it along, probably believing he wouldn't know. But Mace knew. It was part of his inherent survival instinct. Not to mention, his experience.

Why did she feel compelled to carry it in the first place? He didn't know many women who carried weapons unless they were law enforcement. So why Colby? Did she feel unsafe around him, or was there some other reason?

That would be something he would have to look into if—*when*—he got to know her better. And on that note, nothing like the present to get started... "Are you planning on filling up these rooms?"

He forced down another bite of delicious salad, then glanced up in time to catch Colby licking chicken juice off her finger with the pointy tip of her tongue. Something suddenly throbbed, and it wasn't his leg.

He'd probably scare the shit out of her if she knew how hard he was at the moment. He needed to be patient. Patience was one virtue he did have since he worked undercover. He could manipulate and "work" almost any situation to his favor. However, he wasn't on the job right now, and his cock begged for release.

"I attend estate auctions whenever I can, along with the occasional antiquing. I think that's the best way to find furniture to match this house. Don't you?"

He blew out a breath, clearing his thoughts. It was a struggle to stay on the topic at hand, and he fought the urge to suggest them doing something besides talking. Something more along the lines of getting naked.

"That's not what I meant. I meant fill it up with family, with kids." Talking about the future, family, and kids was enough to get his horniness under control. Somewhat. He'd take what he could get.

"Oh." Colby picked up a paper napkin to wipe her lips. "Someday, I guess."

Okay, then. Most women dreamed of their own home and filling it with family, right? Why not her? She didn't seem to care about the family part. Maybe she was too independent. Though that "now" part really nagged at the back of his mind. But he didn't want to push his luck and make her clam up.

After packing up the cooler and collecting the garbage, she pushed herself to her feet, wiping her hands on her overalls. "Ready to help me finish painting the kitchen?"

To be honest, he wasn't. His leg ached. He'd rather sit back and watch her body move as she swept the walls with bright yellow paint like an artist on a canvas.

And his painting wasn't nearly as neat as hers. After the first few smears, she insisted on him rolling the center of the walls while she brushed the edges. He admired her though; she worked hard and never complained. He wanted to complain but kept his mouth shut, determined to stick it out as long as she did.

THE RECEDING light in the kitchen signaled that the sun was falling below the horizon. Colby stood in the center of the now bright yellow room, studying their efforts. Mace found much better things to stare at, like her fiery hair spattered with yellow paint. Her body was reed-like even though she had matched his appetite bite for bite at lunch, and her delicate wrists and long, slender fingers had been fascinating to watch while she'd been applying the paint. It amazed him she wore no jewelry except a very small pair of gold studs in her ears. Though her hair was the best accessory she could have. Jewelry couldn't do her justice next to that mass of crimson fire—fire he wanted to burn all over his body.

The thought of stripping her naked and fucking her hard on the drop cloth engulfed him. He turned away so she wouldn't see the noticeable bulge in his jeans. Normally, he could control his urges, but it had been a while since he'd been around a female like Colby. Sort of innocent, unjaded. A woman not involved in illegal activities, not shady at all.

Refreshing.

And best of all, she didn't make the hair on the back of his neck stand up.

"What do you think? I think it looks great." When Mace didn't answer, she continued. "Just wait until the new appliances come in, and the new counter tops. I hope yellow was the right choice."

Insecurity laced her voice. For some reason, her life seemed to depend on something as simple as whether she made the right choice in paint color. If sunshine yellow wasn't the perfect match for the new sink and countertops, she would be devastated.

"If it's not, we can repaint it." Not that he really wanted to volunteer for that, but— Complete silence enveloped him. He turned to glance at her. Her expression of horror concerned him; it was almost as if she took it as a personal attack. He moved behind her to place his palms on her shoulders and rubbed them softly. "The yellow looks great," he assured her, then trailed his hands up her neck, his thumbs stroking the slender muscles under the soft skin.

Her smile returned as quickly as it disappeared, but she pulled away from his touch and walked out of the room. She chattered away about the wall colors of the other rooms. Mace shook his head and sighed. She was either oblivious or trying to ignore the fact some spark existed between them.

But one thing was clear; she was burying herself in this house for a reason. Probably the same reason she added the "now" to her *she could take care of herself* declaration. There was a fresh wound there somewhere. Physical, mental, he couldn't tell yet.

Of course people took pride in their homes, but she seemed a little too fixated. And he wanted to know why.

CHAPTER 3

MACE ENDED up sleeping through most of Sunday morning after finding a note, during an early morning bladder relief run, that Colby left on the bathroom door. The message stated she went to an estate sale with a friend, and they were hitting some yard sales on the way. Oh, and she hoped he didn't mind her borrowing his truck. Well, hell. That was pretty ballsy of her

At the same time, Colby absconding with his truck gave him an excuse to crawl back into bed. Now, a couple hours later and still feeling lazy, he remained buried under his covers. If she had been smart, she would have slept in, too. Hell, if *he* was smart, he would have woken up with her in his arms, preferably naked, and started the day off right. But no. Instead, he lay in his bed by himself; his only company his morning, or more like mid-morning, wood.

He slid a hand down past the elastic of his boxer briefs and straightened out his hard-on. Damn. Doing it himself just wasn't the same. It was like settling for an after-dinner mint when you really wanted a piece of chocolate silk pie.

But since Colby was gone, he wasn't left with any other option. Rolling toward his nightstand, he came face-to-face with the photo of his late parents. He cursed and slammed the framed picture facedown. Just what he needed: his parents watching him relieve some sexual tension. As a teen, he'd worried enough about them catching him. Though never quite caught in the act, there had been some close calls. Too many to count.

Thankfully for his cock this morning, it wasn't a concern anymore. He yanked open the drawer and shoved his hand deep until his fingers bumped against a small box. He pulled it out—condoms—and turned it over and read the expiration date. Hell, these were so old, not to mention probably so dry, they would break just trying to roll them on. Useless. He'd need to stock up next time he ran errands. He planned on needing fresh ones. Maybe he could just add them to Colby's grocery list, the narrow pad of paper attached to the fridge by a magnet. Milk, eggs, bread, condoms. Yeah, that might be a tip-off.

The box ended up tossed next to the picture frame, and he continued his search. *Ah, success.*

With a sigh of relief, he lifted out the tube of water-soluble lube. He smirked. Relief was what he needed and relief was what he would get. He swore he'd had a perpetual erection since returning home the other day and coming face-to-face with a redheaded woman.

What was worse, every time he tried to touch her, even innocently enough, she pulled away. He was getting nowhere fast. He thought maybe volunteering to help her out at that horrendous house would soften her up to him a bit. And he guessed it had somewhat, but not enough. Not quickly enough for his liking, anyway.

He lifted his hips and slid out of his underwear, tossing it over the fallen picture frame. No risk of peeking for the parents. After plumping his pillows behind him, he sat up to lean against the headboard. *That was more like it.*

With a flick of his finger, the lip on the tube popped open, and he squirted a healthy amount on his palm. His cock bounced against his lower belly in anticipation. He threw the tube aside in his haste, grabbed his cock with his slick hand, and squeezed.

The head turned deep red, and the vein running down his shaft throbbed. He squeezed harder until the crown turned almost purple and then, only then, did he slide his hand up. He ran his thumb around the crown until it was well lubed. He fisted it, sliding his tight grip all the way back down to the base of his shaft.

Holy shit. A slight shudder rolled through him. He couldn't remember the last time he jerked off.

Closing his eyes, he leaned his head back against the headboard, blowing out a shaky breath. He'd only stroked it once. Just one stroke and he wanted to blow his load already. He adjusted his grip, making sure every finger encircled his girth, before stroking slowly once again.

It was Colby he wanted on top of him right now straddling him, pressing her tight, plump, wet lips around his cock. Sliding up and down. *Up. Down.*

Gliding his hand faster along his length, he kept a steady, smooth rhythm. Even though his fist felt slick and warm, he rather it be her riding him, slamming her ass cheeks against his lap, taking every inch of him and asking for more. *Fuck.*

Tightening his fist, he quickened his pace. Up to the edge of the crown, a squeeze, then a solid stroke back down. His balls tightened with the urge to come in her pussy. Her ass, her mouth, hell, he didn't care.

Repeating his stroke, over and over, he lifted his hips with each downward motion and pushed against the mattress with each upstroke.

His chest heaved, trying to catch his breath. He was close. So close. He grabbed the root of his cock harder and squeezed all the way to the top. Then down once more. On the last upstroke, a throaty groan escaped his lips while hot cum spurted all over his stomach and chest. He leaned back, panting, unable to move, his cock twitching with release. Squeezing it one last time, he milked it of any remaining fluid.

A soft chuckle escaped him. He'd needed that and would have to do it again sometime soon. He padded to the bathroom naked, only a slight limp hindering him due to his self-indulgent actions. Sometime soon became there and now. While he showered, he soaped himself up and gave himself another hand job, a little more leisurely this time.

He finally dragged himself out of the shower when the water turned cool. With a large towel wrapped around his waist, he stepped out into the hall—and smacked right into Colby.

They both jumped back in surprise, Colby squealed an "oh" at the same time Mace apologized.

"Sorry, sorry. I didn't see you there. Are you okay?" *Fuck!* Had she heard him whacking off in the shower?

If so, she showed no signs of it. She stepped back and gave him a shaky smile, her hand over her heart. "I'm fine. I should have been more careful."

"No, my fault." Lack of oxygen to the brain. More like lack of blood.

She turned slightly and stepped back again, pinning herself against the hallway wall. Was she uncomfortable because he only sported a towel? He checked it to make sure it wouldn't slip off. Yes, he wanted her, but not enough to just drop the thing in the middle of the hallway and offer himself up.

He cleared his throat, and his thoughts before the towel rose at attention. "How was your bargain hunting?"

"Oh, uh, good. We had fun. I found a couple of nice small tables at the estate auction and picked up a few kitchen items at the yard sales."

"So, the truck came in handy?"

Color rushed up her chest to her throat. "I'm sorry. I should have asked. The keys were down by the front door, and I didn't want to wake you. I filled up your tank."

"Hey, no problem. At least you left a note."

. . .

COLBY TRIED to avoid staring at Mace's chest. It was just like she imagined it would be. Sculpted, but not too hard. Just right. He had small, dark nipples peeking out from a dusting of dark hair. A trail of hair circled his belly button and disappeared into the towel. No six-pack but damn well close enough.

His damp hair, long enough to almost brush his shoulders, curled slightly around his face. She clenched her fingers into fists, fighting the urge to comb through it.

She studied the angle of his jaw, the curve of his upper lip, and the edge of his brow before meeting his eyes. She realized he just stood quietly, waiting for her to finish checking him out. *Shit.* How long had they stood there without saying a word? The heat, already licking at her throat, rose into her cheeks.

When he reached out, she automatically flinched. He hesitated a long second, then brushed his knuckles over her cheekbone. Even though his expression stayed neutral, she caught the quick curiosity in his eyes before he schooled that as well. Her face became even hotter. She couldn't believe her own fear of a touch that ended up being so gentle.

"No reason to be embarrassed."

She opened her mouth to tell him she wasn't, but instead, she said nothing. He couldn't know her blush wasn't from the physical contact but her humiliating instinctive reaction to his sudden movement toward her instead.

When he moved closer, only a breath away, she backed against the wall, wishing she could disappear into the drywall. He wore a towel. *Only a towel.* Even though it was long enough to cover him practically to his knees, one little slip, and he would be totally naked.

She licked her dry lips, and the motion drew his gaze. With lowered lids, he ran a thumb along her jawline, then over her freshly moistened bottom lip.

His face lowered until just inches away. "Can I kiss you?"

Colby swallowed hard, but the lump in her throat remained. "I don't think that's a good idea."

"Why not?"

His hot breath mingled with hers. As if their life breath was already intimate, kissing each other. "We don't know each other that well."

"A kiss might remedy the situation."

She shook her head slightly, still captivated by how close he was. If she shifted, their lips would touch. "I don't want things to be uncomfortable between us. We share a roof right now. A kiss might...complicate things."

"It's just a kiss. A simple, quick kiss. Two people putting their lips together."

Somehow, she didn't think it would be so simple. Or quick.

She reached out to push him away; she needed some breathing space, some clarity for her boggled brain. But when she did, her fingers encountered his heated skin, his muscles, the light, wiry hair along his chest.

The contact made her suck in her breath, but when she did, he closed the infinitesimal space between them. His lips brushed hers lightly, then pulled back a breadth. He breathed her in, and she did the same with him. He grazed her lips again. So soft. No pressure at all.

On the third sweep, he grabbed her shoulders and crushed his lips to hers. She opened her mouth to protest, but he slanted his against hers, dipping his tongue in, searching.

She forgot her objection as Mace's tongue invaded her mouth, skimmed along her teeth, and tangled with hers until she groaned and tentatively drew her tongue against his. Their tongues met, dueled and fought, twisting and pushing against each other. Her hands moved up his chest until one clasped his neck, while the other held his head in place, before pulling him even closer. She couldn't get enough of him. He wasn't close enough. Not nearly close enough.

He tasted good. His minty freshness combined with his own flavor. Very male. She couldn't put a finger on what it was, but she savored it.

He slid his hands along her waist, one moving to her lower back, the other to her ass. He pulled her against him so she could feel his erection through the cotton towel, ready and heavy with need. A small sound escaped her, but it became lost within their kiss. When he tilted his hips slightly, his hardness pressed against her lower belly.

Mace slipped his hand from the small of her back to grab her other ass cheek. He gave them a quick squeeze and lifted her without breaking the kiss, pulling her against him.

Panic started to set in and cloud her mind when Colby wanted to rip the towel off and drag him to the floor. This was wrong. Wrong. She had only known him for a couple days at best.

They needed to slow down. Take a breath. This shouldn't be happening.

Colby finally released her tight grip on his hair. She broke the kiss and gasped for breath. He nuzzled her behind the ear when she said, "Stop."

He did. Immediately.

When he released her ass, her heels lowered to the floor until she stood on her own. He shifted slightly but didn't back away. He tried to capture her gaze, but she turned her head away.

"You didn't enjoy that?"

"No…Yes…Yes, it was fine. It was…very nice." She couldn't face him yet. Not yet. He remained too close. Too hot. Too tempting.

"Nice?" He caught her chin with his thumb and tilted her head to face him. He wore a lopsided smile. He wasn't being cocky; he actually seemed a little worried about her reaction. And his response alone made her relax.

"Fishing for compliments?" She tried to laugh, but it fell flat.

"Always." He shook his head. "But seriously, I'm sorry if I came on too strong."

She didn't answer. Even though she enjoyed every second, just as he did, she shouldn't have. She shouldn't have. She didn't do these things with strangers.

"Colby—"

The house phone rang, making Colby jump. "The phone."

"Yes, I recognize the sound. Ignore it."

"What if it's Maxi?"

"Unlikely, but if it is, she'll call back."

On the fourth ring, she said, "It might be Martin." She slipped past him and hurried into her room. She climbed across her bed to reach the one of the few phones remaining in the house. "Hello?" For a moment, dead silence greeted her on the other end. Absolutely nothing. Then she heard breathing. "Hello? Anybody there?"

More loud breathing. The hair on her neck stood up, and she gripped the phone harder. Her heart frantically pounding, she shouted into the phone, "Who is this?"

Mace snatched the phone out of her hand. "Hello?" A second later, he slammed it down on the receiver. He stared at the cordless phone for a long moment, a muscle jumping in his tight jaw, before turning to her. "Must have been a wrong number." He blew out a breath and dragged a hand through his hair. "Why is there still a fucking landline in this house?" he muttered to himself.

Though she didn't understand his frustration about the landline issue, he was probably right about the wrong number. No one knew where she lived except for work. Even so, she couldn't stop the tremors.

Without a thought, she leaned past Mace to open the nightstand drawer and check for her gun. She removed it and yanked back the slide to make sure a round sat in the chamber.

"What the hell? You had more clips?" Mace ripped the gun out of her hand and put it back in the drawer, slamming it shut. "Colby, answer me."

"Yes. Of course." She glanced toward the closed drawer. She needed her gun in her hands right now, needed to feel the security it gave her. But a big man stood between her and her Glock.

"What are you going to do? Shoot the phone? It was a wrong number, that's all," he said in a more soothing voice.

He was right, he was right, he was right. She was being stupid. It could be as simple as a kid prank calling or just a wrong number. She was making more out of it than necessary. She focused on the man in front of her. "Sorry. You're right. I'm just being…" Crazy. Paranoid. "Silly."

He settled on the bed next to her and reached for her hand. Though she wanted him to grab her and hold her tight, make her feel safe and secure, she also didn't want him getting closer to her. She didn't want to rely on him or anyone. She was responsible for her own life and her own actions now.

The only one who could protect her was…well, herself.

She stood and slipped her hand out of his. Backing up a step toward the bedroom door, she couldn't resist one more look at him. He was so sexy on her bed in just a towel. If she wanted him, she could have him in a second. After the kiss in the hallway, she was sure if she suggested they get naked, he wouldn't think twice about tossing the towel to the side.

No doubt she needed some uncomplicated loving, some tenderness, and maybe even some hot, sweaty, down-and-dirty sex, but it wasn't her priority.

Right now, she needed to survive, needed to get out of the bedroom. "I'm going downstairs to start a roast." She turned and fled down the hall.

In her haste, she barely heard Mace's disgruntled question. "By the way, who's Martin?"

CHAPTER 4

MACE WAS towel-drying his hair Monday morning when the shrill ring of his cell phone cut through the air. He could work highly technical surveillance equipment, but he couldn't even figure out how to change the damn ringtone. Not that he had given it any great effort. Especially after dealing mostly with burner phones for the past couple years.

He limped into the bedroom and looked at the "private caller" which came up on the display. He reluctantly answered it before the voicemail could pick up.

"So, how are you feeling?" a very familiar male voice asked.

Mace sat on the bed and threw the damp towel over his naked lap. "Lousy. Are you calling for a reason?"

"Not really. I'm just checking on one of my best men. Did you shave that mess off your face yet?"

"No." Mace rubbed a hand over his stubbled chin. "I like it. I think I'll keep it for a while."

"It makes you look—"

"Like a criminal. I've already heard. Flattery will get you everywhere. Hey, did you call the house phone yesterday?" It would be like his boss to hang up if a stranger's voice answered. To avoid any questions, his superior would say.

"I have your cell."

Yeah, that was the perfect answer. But he was right. He had Mace's cell, there would be no reason to call the house.

"Is there a problem, Walker?"

"No. No, nothing." Nothing but some kiddies prank calling the house.

"If there is, I'm sure it's something you can handle."

"Yeah. In that case, I'm glad you waited until now to call. There's a woman staying here. Fortunately, she's at work right now."

"I know. You're speaking of Ms. Colby Parks."

Mace gripped the phone tighter. "You know?"

"Of course. I wouldn't let you walk unknowingly into a situation which might be dangerous."

"Don't make me laugh. Everything I do, every situation you send me into, is dangerous." Mace glanced at the full gun clip still sitting on his nightstand. He picked it up and studied it. Out of habit, he pushed the top round with his thumb, testing the tightness of the clip's spring. It was a motion he'd done thousands of times; for some reason, it comforted him. "Speaking of dangerous, she almost shot me thinking I was a burglar. It would have been nice if you'd warned me."

He thought he heard a chuckle, or it might just have been choking, on the other end. "It wouldn't have been any fun, though. Maybe she'll keep you on your toes, keep you from getting fat and lazy during your little recuperation." His next response was dead serious. "I checked her out."

"Now why doesn't that surprise me? Actually, you beat me to it. I was going to call the Bureau today." He placed the clip next to the framed pictured of his parents. "So you know my sister married and is on her honeymoon?"

"Yes. She married over a month ago. She told me, but I couldn't pass that on to you. Simply bad timing. First, you were too deep undercover. And then with your little mishap, well, I didn't want you to be bothered."

Little mishap.

"Right." Mace gave a dry laugh. "Do you at least know who she married, where she went?"

No matter how many times he'd tried to coax the information out of Colby, she'd clam up and tell him to find out for himself. She believed if Maxi wanted him to know, she would have told him. Which was untrue. He wanted to explain it had to do with the circumstances of his career, but Mace decided it wasn't worth arguing over. He had to pick his battles, and he preferred the one where he worked on getting her comfortable enough with him to get naked.

Priorities.

He smiled at the image. But his boss' voice broke into his thoughts, ruining his fantasy.

"Of course. I know everything. She married the banker who backed Ms. Parks' atrocious project, the one on Shady Lane. That's how your sister met Ms. Parks. Do you like her?"

Mace ignored the question. "She's horrifying with a gun."

"A Glock—"

"Yeah, yeah, yeah. You know everything. You're too thorough."

"I have to be. Our lives depend on it, Walker. I assume you don't want me to tell you everything about her. A mysterious woman can be so much more…intriguing." Papers rustled on the other end of the line. "I hope you'll keep up your physical therapy—and I don't mean naked romper room with Ms. Parks. Try to heal quickly. I might need you to replace another agent on assignment. He's getting too personally involved."

"A woman?"

"Mmm. Unfortunately, she's on the wrong side."

"A fatal mistake," Mace said. "But, of course, *you know that.* If possible, I'd like to stick around for a couple months."

"Until your sister returns from abroad?"

"Is that where she is?"

"Yes, her new husband has family in England. They decided to tour Europe." The man laughed. "It has to be you want to wait around to see your sister. I can't imagine you'd want to stay just to help Ms. Parks fix up her ugly, old house."

"It really isn't so bad." Did he actually just say that?

"And she's worth it even if it is, right? Maybe she'll help you feel better. Have her help with your PT exercises." His boss chuckled.

Perhaps a couple months around Colby would make him feel better. If she was willing. "Does Maxi even know what happened?"

A telling silence answered him. Of course not, otherwise his baby sister wouldn't have gone off to Europe. She would have been worried sick. She would have put off her wedding, put her life on hold. Maybe it was better Maxi didn't know.

The man cleared his throat. "I'll keep in touch."

Mace stared at the cell for a moment as it went dark, and then he tossed it on the bed.

Now that he knew his boss hadn't called yesterday, he thought about Colby's reaction. Why was she all shook up from one hang-up? Okay two; there had been one later in the evening. But he got to the phone first, and it had been just a quick click and a dial tone.

Mace played the second one off as another wrong number since Colby had been within earshot. He ended up telling her someone was trying to order Chinese food and had misdialed. Whether she believed him or not, who knew, but at least she hadn't freaked like the last time.

When he'd asked her whether the hang-ups had been a reoccurring thing before he'd come home, she changed the subject. He let it go. For now. But he would get to the bottom of it one way or another.

LATE IN THE AFTERNOON, Mace heard a car drive up and opened the front door to see who it was. He surprised himself; he never even looked out the peephole first. It felt good to open a door without fear of some thug blowing holes in him. Three days home, and he was starting to relax already.

Colby parked a bright red, but older, convertible next to his not so bright, old Ford truck. He spotted the groceries in the back seat and went to help her.

"Sharp," he said, snagging a couple of the bags.

Colby handed him a third and grabbed one herself. "Me or the car?"

"Both. I didn't think you had a vehicle."

"It was at the garage. Needed a water pump."

He followed her into the house. "Yeah? Too bad I didn't arrive sooner. I'm great with cars."

"And women?" she tossed over her shoulder.

He grinned. "Them too."

"Did you learn your mechanical skills at—"

Mace dropped the grocery bags on the kitchen table in time to cover her mouth with his hand. "Don't. I've had enough of your jailhouse wisecracks."

His fingers against her warm, moist lips immediately sent a shock wave down to his groin. He wanted to run his thumb along her bottom lip and then dip it in and out of her mouth until it was wet. He would follow his thumb with his tongue. And other things. Or just one other thing: his aching, swollen cock. His eyelids lowered with need until Colby stepped away from him, breaking his contact, breaking into his thoughts.

"Too close to home?" she asked, her voice a little shaky.

Good. Maybe he affected her like she affected him. "No."

"So, tell me what you do for a living."

He broke eye contact first, because if he hadn't, he would have pushed her Miss Proper skirt up and slammed his cock home very improper-like against the kitchen cabinet. Frontward, backward, he wouldn't be picky.

Instead, he concentrated hard on the subject at hand. "You first. What do you do with your days, *Ms. Parks?*"

"You're avoiding the question. Finish carrying in the groceries while I unpack them, and then, and only then, I might play your little game, Mr. Walker."

If she only knew what game he really wanted to play with her...

He behaved himself and brought in the rest of the bags. Settling into a chair, he regarded Colby while she started dinner.

"Are you an MCP?"

A what? He shot her a questioning look.

"A male chauvinist pig," she clarified. "Don't you cook or clean or do laundry?"

Mace smiled. "I try to avoid it at all costs."

"So, who normally does all your domestic duties?"

"Here we go with the questions again. You still need to answer mine."

She gave a little shrug. "Fine."

He stood and moved in behind Colby. She started when she turned around and found him so close. Close enough to feel her heat. And make him lose his mind.

"What are you doing?"

The tremble in her voice caught his attention and threw a little cold water on his steaming hot libido. "Helping. I assume that's what you wanted when you started in on the male chauvinist crap."

When her relief was obviously clear, Mace shook his head. Three days had gone by. They'd eaten meals and watched TV together, and he had even helped her paint her yellow kitchen. Not to mention the make-out session in the hallway yesterday. But she still hadn't relaxed around him yet.

Thinking about their up-close and personal time on Sunday made his cock snap right back up to attention. But he needed to be cautious. Even though he wanted to get down and dirty with her, discover all her secrets, he couldn't push too hard. Not yet. He didn't want to scare her away. Hell, if he wasn't careful, the sexual tension would kill him.

"You've read my mind. You can make the salad."

If they were reading each other's minds, he was in trouble. Because right now, his mind was dirty, dirty, so fucking filthy. He imagined digging his fingers deep into her fireball mane while she sucked him off. She would be on her knees, and he would be guiding her head back and forth. Her wet mouth around his cock, little moans escaping her lips...

Mace bit off a groan and removed the rinsed vegetables out of the colander where they'd been drip-drying. He grabbed a cutting board and sat back down at the table to chop them. He had to concentrate on something else. Like lettuce.

"Can't you do that here at the counter?"

"No. Sometimes, I can't stand on my leg too long."

Her eyes raked him, then settled on his legs. Damn. He wished it were her hands following the lines of his jeans instead. She wasn't helping him get his mind out of the gutter.

"Why?"

He cocked an eyebrow in her direction.

She raised her palms up in surrender. "Okay, I'll tell you about me first." After Colby placed two thick steaks on the broiler pan and got some baby red potatoes boiling, she turned to face him, leaning back against the counter. At least she seemed a bit more comfortable now. "I'm a biochemist."

"Impressive." He clumsily peeled a carrot, attempting to keep the long orange strips in a pile. Concentrating on the vegetables helped to relieve some of the tension within him. "What's that?" He glanced up from his detested work when he heard her laugh.

Hands planted on her hips, she gave him a look of surprise. "How could something impress you when you don't know what it is?"

"That's why I'm impressed. I never said I was smart."

"I thought all inmates had a right to an education." She raised her hands up in surrender again at his grimace. "Sorry. I promise, no more digs." She grabbed the dishtowel which hung over the oven door handle and wiped her hands, then she drifted over to the table and snagged a stalk of celery to munch on. "I specialize in the chemical composition and behavior of living organisms. I work for Malvern University."

If she was trying to dumbfound him, she succeeded. He couldn't have felt any dumber. "Can you elaborate a little more? I think you lost me."

"I study the effects of food or hormones, or even drugs, on living things."

Ah. "Like people?" *I could tell you about the effects of drugs on people.*

"People, animals, plants. Whatever." She pointed the ragged stub of celery in his direction. "Whatever the University wants me to do, I do. They're the ones paying my salary."

"I bet it's a pretty nice salary too."

"It could be better. I only have my Masters. To earn more, I'd need my Ph.D."

Only has her Masters. Right. "Are you considering it?" He took the salad bowls Colby handed him and filled them with the unevenly chopped veggies. "Going back to school, I mean."

"No. I enjoy working in the lab and in the field. I don't want an administrative position. No matter how much they earn."

"I can understand that. I wouldn't want to be stuck behind a desk either." Mace caught the towel Colby tossed to him and wiped his hands. "How did you get to work this morning? I would have given you a ride. The University isn't very close."

"Martin, my assistant. He was kind enough to pick me up this morning and drop me off at the garage after work. He's a nice guy."

"Just nice, huh?" Mace wondered if there was more. He waited, but she said nothing else about her co-worker.

Malvern University. When he said he was impressed, he meant it. It was a prestigious school. His parents had moved to this college "town" when he and Maxi were young. Their professor father taught

48

there until he died. Maxi also got her degree there. Mace had different ideas when he went to college; he found the farthest school from home in the lower forty-eight. Like he could have gotten into Malvern in the first place—

"So, what's with the leg?" Colby asked, jolting him back to the present.

"I was shot." Her question had come so unexpectedly, he answered before he could think about it. *Damn.*

Her brows lifted in surprise. "So you weren't kidding? What, in a prison riot?" The color in her cheeks darkened when she realized what she said. "I'm sorry. If you would just tell me what you do for a living, I'd stop."

"Why is it so important? What if I just like to travel around like a bum?"

"Why would you want to when you have a nice home here?"

"I don't know. I get bored?"

"No. I don't know what you're hiding, but I won't tell anyone. Promise." She crossed her fingers and made an X with them over her heart.

Mace smiled at the gesture. He wanted to trust her. He really did. But after years and years of getting good at lies, the truth didn't come so easily. It was difficult to step back into his "real life." Or what he thought should be his real life.

"Can I see your leg?"

Once again, her question caught him off guard. Mace put down the paring knife he absently played with before he accidentally sliced off his finger. Did she want him to pull his pants down in the middle of the kitchen before dinner? Not that he minded getting naked for her, but he wanted to show her something besides his injury.

As if she read his mind, she quipped, "I don't mean now. Later."

"I thought you were a scientist. Not a doctor."

"I'm still interested. A scientist is interested in all living things. And in this particular instance, I'm interested how metal affects human flesh."

"Not very well, I can attest to that. It hurts and looks like hell. But if you really want to see it, you have to promise to kiss it and make it better."

She probably thought he joked. He didn't. He believed if she would only place her sweet, luscious lips on his healing leg, all the hurt might disappear. Hell, it was worth a try.

"I promise." She laughed.

Mace joined in her laughter. Little did she know, he would make her keep her promise. "Tell me more about this Martin."

She gave him her back. "He's a nice guy I work with."

And spent last Sunday morning with him at an auction and bargain hunting. Who knows what else. "Yeah, you already said that."

"That about covers it."

COLBY GLANCED up from the sitcom she watched. The popcorn bowl balanced on her lap tilted dangerously. Luckily, she caught it in time and placed it on the coffee table which sat in front of the couch. "Oh, my God."

Mace limped across the den toward her wearing a pair of cut-off denim shorts. And nothing else. "I told you it wasn't pretty."

"Who did this to you?" she whispered. She reached out when he neared, wanting to touch, but unsure.

Without hesitation, he stepped into her touch, his eyes sliding closed. "Be gentle with me."

Colby glanced up to see if he teased. He didn't. Pain etched across his face, muscles flexed in his jaw, and she returned her attention to his leg, pushing the denim higher to get a better look. His thigh looked like little more than hamburger meat. Half of his inner thigh muscle was missing, and she could see the outline of his thighbone under the skin. Red seam-like scars remained where the doctors had sewn the skin together.

It must have been a hell of a big gun. She bit her lip, wondering how he could have endured the pain. "You're lucky it wasn't amputated." Colby didn't realize she spoke out loud until she heard his snort and bitter words.

His dark eyes opened to bore into her. "I'm lucky the gun wasn't pointed a few more inches to the left. I would have been missing something a little more important than a thigh muscle."

He gritted his teeth and a bead of sweat appeared on his forehead when she cautiously, but lightly, stroked the angry red skin with her fingertips. It seemed even the softest touch bothered him. Surprisingly, he didn't pull away or tell her to stop.

"Sorry if I'm not very receptive to your touch right now. Normally, I'd be at full attention."

Colby immediately glanced at the V of his shorts before looking away, heat crawling up her neck. She had fallen right into his trap. "What I see you popping all the time…Are they painkillers?"

"Do you blame me?"

"No. But there are other ways to ease pain. Natural ways."

"If you're talking about holistic medicine, forget it. I'll stick to the good ol' American way of popping a pill for every ache." Mace dropped on the couch beside her, dislodging her hand. He propped his leg on the table and picked up the remote control. "What are you watching?"

Colby snagged the remote out of his hands and shut the television off. She tossed it out of his reach onto the recliner a few feet away. "No way. You're not getting out of this so easily. I want to know who did this and why."

"Well, the why is easy. I'm sure a rocket—I mean, biological—scientist can even figure that one out. He was trying to kill me."

"Who? Why?" Why would anyone be trying to kill this man?

His hand dug harshly through his hair, leaving it mussed. "I can't tell you the details, Colby, even if I wanted to." He grabbed a random magazine from the coffee table and thumbed through it before tossing it restlessly back onto the table.

"Are you a cop?"

Mace shook his head and glanced longingly over at the remote.

"Are you in the armed forces?"

"No." He gazed up at the ceiling and blew out a long breath.

"Am I going to have to play twenty questions with you?"

"No, but I can tell you this." He twisted toward her and pinned her with a stare. "I work for the FBI."

"Do you go undercover? Is that why you haven't had contact with Maxi for two years?" Maybe he was undercover now. Who was he really? Was she in the middle of some sort of sting? Her heart raced.

Mace groaned. "Colby, please don't ask details. I can't tell you, and it's better if you don't know, anyway."

She turned to study his face. "Are you really Macen Walker, or is this some kind of alias? Are you really Maxi's brother?"

He rolled his eyes and snorted. "Yes, I'm who I said I was. I thought we went through this the first night."

Colby suddenly felt horrible about the way she treated him in the beginning. "I thought you were a criminal! And here you are risking your life—"

He placed a finger over her lips. "Shhh."

She jerked her head away and narrowed her eyes. "No, don't shush me. I'm sorry. I'm sorry for thinking you were a...a..."

"Colby, it's all right. I'm a big boy; I can take a little ribbing."

"No, it's not all right. You're in constant pain. And don't lie and say you aren't. I wondered why you limped every once in a while. Why you struggle to do something as easy as walk up the stairs."

Tears stung her eyes. But she wouldn't cry. No. She didn't want to appear like an overemotional baby.

Damn it. She tried to catch a runaway tear, but it escaped before she could brush it away.

MACE CAUGHT the tear on his finger and stared at it. He had to admit, Colby's emotion touched him. No one but his sister had really cared about him in a long time. Or cared what happened to him. An unfamiliar ache swelled in his chest.

But he didn't want to do this right now. He couldn't do this. He didn't want to open up an emotional Cracker Jack box. He'd only known this woman for a few days. He really needed his sister. She was the reason he'd come home. He needed an emotional and a physical Band-Aid.

"Don't cry for me, Colby. I survived. Otherwise, we'd never have met. For some reason, I feel we can help each other right now. I'm trying to heal, and I think you are too, in some way."

Colby shook her head but avoided his gaze.

Mace grasped her chin and turned her to look deeply into her eyes. "Yes, you're dealing with something. Some kind of pain of your own. I think it's the reason why you're so involved with your house. Every little thing about that house seems to be a crisis that needs solving." He stroked his thumb over her cheek. He caught her teary gaze before lowering his voice to just above a whisper. "Why? What happened to you, Colby Parks?"

"N-nothing."

He didn't believe her. She had been hurt—maybe not like him, physically—but possibly mentally or emotionally. Not just hurt, but hurt badly. He had been hurt by people who hated him, couldn't care less about him. He assumed she had been hurt by someone she loved. Or cared for. Someone close to her.

Her reddened eyes matched the tip of her nose. A couple more tears ran unchecked down her cheeks. He desperately wanted to lean over and kiss those tears away. He wanted to haul her against him and take her into his arms, to hold her until the demons were squeezed out of them both. He wanted to lose himself in her and just feel, forget everything else but the two of them. But he didn't want to overwhelm her either since he was so desperate for her touch. He didn't trust himself if he reached out first. She had to make the first move.

And, surprisingly, she did.

Colby brushed the back of her fingers along his whiskered chin. Tilting her head, she followed her hand with her eyes.

Mace reached up and grasped her fingers, bringing them to his lips. "You promised to kiss it and make it feel better. I can understand if you don't want to. It's pretty hideous."

She shook her head slightly. Then, she stared at his misshapen thigh for a few seconds before leaning down and placing her warm lips gently against his skin.

Mace leaned back, closing his eyes. His hands dug into her hair, gripping her braid firmly. As her lips fluttered to different areas of his thigh, he released a groan. She turned her face and rubbed her soft cheek against his scarred skin.

"Oh, God, Colby. Don't stop," he whispered brokenly. "Please don't stop."

She turned her face again until her other cheek rested on his leg. She gazed up at him. Mace opened his eyes, staring back. Her tears had stopped, and she looked and felt so good lying across his lap. He wanted to stay that way forever, but his body had other ideas.

He took her hand, which gripped his good thigh, and moved it over slightly until she could feel how much he wanted her. Damn, did he want her. He wanted to plunge deep and hard into her softness and just lose himself within her.

Colby's fingers closed around him through the soft, worn denim of his shorts, and he thrust upward. His breathing deepened, and his head fell back against the couch. "Colby..." He swallowed hard. "Let me go if you don't want this to continue. It's been a while since—"

"For me, too."

Her words caused hot lightning to shoot to through his body. He hooked his hands behind her elbows and drew her up, though she carefully avoided his bad thigh.

Mace rolled the elastic band off the end of her French braid and released the strands of hair one by one. Her breathing shallowed, and her nipples pebbled, ready for his touch—by his tongue, his lips, and his hands. With her hair free, he spread her deep-red mane around her shoulders and held a few strands to his nostrils, inhaling the sweet scent he now recognized as hers. *"Fuck.* I want your hair draped all over my body. I want to feel the silkiness against my skin."

He slowly unbuttoned her blouse until it hung open, exposing her white, lacy bra. Her large, dark nipples were visible through the delicate fabric—just enough to drive him mad. He drew a finger along the edges, barely touching her skin. And when she arched her back, he couldn't resist releasing them and unclasped her bra. *Perfect.* Round and full, puckered with need.

A gentle brush of a finger over one dark tip made her squirm and whisper his name. She reached up and delved her hands into his hair, and then pulled his face toward her. And with that move, she showed him what she wanted, what she desired.

Mace flicked his tongue over one peak, then the other. Slowly, he drew a nipple into his mouth, savoring the taste as Colby gripped his head tightly, holding him in place. She tilted her head back to give him unfettered access. And using the advantage, he sucked one deep into his mouth, then the other, over and over until she bucked against him and cried out.

Her soft mewing sounds turned his cock to steel. He was surprised to find how shaken his control was. "Colby, I don't know if I can—"

She pressed her lips against his, stopping his words. He savored her sweet mouth, nipping her lower lip. His tongue dipped in, swirling against hers.

His fingers dug into her hips. He wanted her on top, straddling him. He needed her hot pussy pressed against his cock, even if a layer of clothes separated them.

As he eased her closer, he stiffened and cursed. "Damn it!" He leaned back, breaking their contact. Though he attempted to laugh it off, he failed miserably. His thigh cramping caused sharp pain to shoot through the rest of his body. He dropped his head. In regret. In embarrassment. In frustrating unmet need. *Fuck.*

"I'm sorry. There's one feeling which overcomes desire, and it's pain."

Colby shifted away from him, her eyelids still heavy from need. "Are you all right?"

"No." He clenched his fingers into a fist, cursing again. "You don't know how much I want you right now."

"I know, I know." She brushed his hair off his forehead. "We've got to take it slow. Maybe it's better this way."

"No, it's not, believe me. I've got two places that ache. One we can ease. The other we can't. The problem is the one we can't rules my life right now."

"Should I get your pills?" She stood, refastening her bra and closing her shirt.

Mace bit back a scream. Not from the pain, but from frustration due to the apparent hurt on her face. From having to give up, when he was so close to fucking the hell out of this beautiful woman.

Damn the bastard who shot him. Hopefully, he rotted in Hell where he sent him—on a one-way ticket.

He didn't argue when Colby helped him up the stairs and into his room. He lay on his bed, clenching the comforter, his thigh muscle going into spasms. Trying not to shout every curse in the book, he ground his teeth instead. He didn't like to lose control of a situation, and he'd be damned if he would let this pain control him. Control his life.

He blew out a breath in relief when Colby returned with a glass of water. She grabbed the pills from his dresser and, after reading the label, gave him two. She sat down by his side and waited until the spasms subsided.

A few minutes later, Mace unclenched his jaw enough to thank her. "Do you need me to help you undress?"

"No. I think you've helped me enough," he snapped. He instantly regretted his tone when she made a little wounded sound. He grabbed her hand, halting her escape. "Colby, I didn't mean it like that. I'm not mad at you. I'm mad at myself. I appreciate the help you've given me. Believe me, I would love for you to take my clothes off," *and see you with your shirt off again; I would love to suck and lick your breasts, those nipples,* "but not right now. I want us both to enjoy it." He still felt like an ass and didn't want her to leave him just yet. "Please. Stay with me a little while." He patted the bed next to him. "Lie next to me."

Colby gave him a skeptical look.

"C'mon. I'm harmless right now, and it'll make me feel better."

"Maybe for a little while," she said, carefully lying down next to him. She wedged herself against him, her head on his chest.

This woman fit perfectly in his arms. Warm, soft. Perfect. His breathing deepened, and before he knew it, he was asleep.

MACE JERKED AWAKE. A heavy weight pressed down on his chest. His hand automatically moved to push it off but connected with hair. And skin. Warm, smooth skin.

He turned his head toward the alarm clock on the nightstand. 12:15. He wiggled his fingers into the plait of her braid, and Colby sighed in her sleep. The room was dark, but he didn't remember turning off the light. Had she? Had she gotten up and turned it off and still felt comfortable enough with him to cuddle up next to him? She had to have gotten up at some point since her hair was back in the tight, controlled braid of hers.

Oh, yeah. Her remaining in his room meant she definitely felt more at ease around him. He didn't mind the dark. Lose one sense and the others make up for it. He might not be able to see her, but he could feel her and smell her sweet scent.

Her head was settled on his chest, her warm breath slipping in and out of her parted lips. It rustled the tiny hairs around his nipple, making it pebble and tighten. Suddenly, he became very aware of where the rest of her body was. Her shoulder was tucked under his armpit, and her breasts pushed into his left side. Her lower body curved away from his legs, probably to not cause him any further pain in his thigh.

With one arm draped over his bare waist, her hand rested on his right hip. He stroked her arm from shoulder to fingertip. He grasped her fingers and slid her palm over his bare lower stomach, letting it settle on the V of hair inversely rising out of his shorts. When her fingers twitched in her sleep, he suddenly found himself very, very hard. And crooked. He adjusted himself, which brought the head of his cock closer to her fingers. So close.

His left arm curled behind her, and he extended his fingers along the small of her back, dipping them into the gap between her shorts and her skin. He spread them until the tips skimmed the top of her ass cheeks. The temptation to stroke along its crevice until he found her tight hole was strong; he guessed it was untouched by any man. Instead, he traced the skin along the edge of her waistband to the front to her belly. He circled his thumb around her navel and, with the third pass, he stretched the rest of his fingers out. They were long enough to slide between her shorts and panties. His fingertips slid along the thin elastic band; he wondered if they were pink satin.

Colby shifted, and her breathing quickened. Little puffs of steam crossed his skin. Either she woke up or her body thought she was in a really, really good dream. He rolled onto his hip, gently laying her on her back and folding her arms over her head onto the pillow. Unable to see if her eyes were open, he drew a thumb along her jawline and then over her parted lips. He swore her tongue licked the pad of his thumb. He dipped his thumb in and…She nipped him. His cock shifted in the tight confines of his boxer briefs, ready to come out to play.

Mace drew one hand down her neck and traced her collarbone—one side and then the other—before he followed the outer curve of her breast. With his other hand, he popped open the button on his shorts and slid the zipper down. After shoving his underwear out of the way, his fingers stroked the head of his cock, slippery with precum. He fisted the head and pushed hard into his palm, arching his hips off the bed.

He stroked himself with long, languid motions while continuing to trace the curve of her breast, making smaller and smaller circles until he found the edge of her areola through her shirt and bra, then pinched the hard center. She gasped and placed a hand on top of his. She didn't say a word. Instead of stopping him, she pushed his hand to her other breast. Her breath broke and a small moan escaped her.

One hand encouraged him to continue his exploration while her other found his hand as it stroked the length of his erection. She worked her fingers underneath his to take control. Her hand might be smaller than his, but, damn, it was a much better choice. She circled the head, collecting the precum, using it to lubricate the rest of his shaft while she fisted his length from root to tip.

Without breaking contact, he settled above her, catching her lips, her warm breath, and her whimpers as he twisted and plucked her hard peaks. Their tongues tangled and fought until they both gasped for air.

He shoved her shirt and bra up over her breasts and replaced his fingers with his mouth on her exposed nipple. He suckled, nudged, and licked until she squirmed. The harder and faster she stroked him, the more precum beaded, making her fist slick like a tight little pussy. He was losing his mind. The more frantically she stroked, the harder he sucked her nipples, until his teeth raked against the hard tip causing her body to shudder against him. She fisted his cock so tightly, he thought the head would pop off.

With a groan, he yanked away and quickly went to his knees between her calves. When he ripped her cotton shorts and panties down, she kicked them free. He shoved his shoulders into the backs of her thighs and pushed them up while spreading them wide, opening her up to him. He wished the light was on; he wanted to see her flushed, plump flesh. Just by feel alone, he could tell she kept herself trimmed, but not shaved; he really wanted to see the fire red hair framing all her glory. *Soon*, he promised himself.

Her luscious scent made him want to come right then and there. Pushing the thought away, he stretched out between her legs. He ran a finger up and down her wet folds, a little deeper each time until the tip of his finger teased her sensitive clit, causing her hips to jerk. He pinned her in place with an arm across her hips.

He sucked her little pleasure button and flicked it, making her squirm. His ran two fingers over her slick folds, and then quickly dipped them in before continuing to her rear. He circled the tight hole, tempted to break that barrier, but he knew it was too soon. So, he slid his fingers deep into her pussy instead while his lips, tongue, and teeth continued to play with her clit.

She whimpered and cried out as her fingers dug into his hair, grabbing tightly, causing pain, clenching and unclenching. He moved down and licked the folds of her labia, his fingers continuing to drive in and out. Even though he held her down, her hips bucked against him, matching every thrust.

At his limit, he couldn't take anymore. His balls became so tight, his cock so hard, it was the most painful pleasure he'd ever experienced. She tugged on his hair, lifting his head up. Grabbing him under the arms, she encouraged him to move over her. He gave her clit a last lingering lick, savoring the taste, and rolled away from her, feeling his way in the dark for the nightstand drawer. He soon found what he was searching for and gave a silent thanks to himself for remembering to buy a new box. He ripped open the condom and rolled it down his length.

Now on his back, his cock stuck straight out from his body. He grabbed her waist with both hands and lifted her up and over him. She settled, straddling his thighs, his cock brushing against her slick skin. She moved forward and slid her pussy along the length of him. The warm folds nestled his balls and rode along his cock until she slowed and paused when the head prodded her opening. She raised herself up, wiggling her hips until the crown lined up perfectly and the tip tucked into her wet heat.

She had finished removing her shirt and bra while he encased himself in latex which allowed him to freely palm the weight of her breasts, pushing them together so the nipples touched. He snagged both tips and rolled them between his fingers and thumbs.

She lowered herself with a moan, burying his cock deep within her. She writhed as he twisted and plucked her nipples The harder he pinched, the deeper she ground herself against him.

He released her nipples to dig his fingers into her ass cheeks, controlling her movements, slowing her down for a moment before reaching beneath her from behind. Her wet folds spread wide, the delicate skin stretched as it engulfed his cock. He stroked a finger along the strip of skin between her pussy and rear, then circled his slick finger around her virgin hole. Once again, temptation pulled at him. He pressed against the tightness, just slightly, seeing if she would encourage him to take that next step.

Her movements became frantic, squeezing his cock with her heated core. Shit, not only was she on the edge, he was too. He stroked her tight rim until she relaxed a bit, then made his move. He slipped a finger in, and she cried out as she convulsed around him, an orgasm rippling through her. With his finger deep in her ass and his cock even deeper within her, he let himself go. He came with a ferocity he hadn't experienced in a long time while her inner muscles milked him dry.

When she collapsed, he tucked her limp body against his. His heart pounded frantically, and his cock still pulsed. He slipped off the condom and wrapped it in a tissue. He'd get rid of it later because he couldn't move even if he tried.

Wiping a hand over his forehead, he blew out a shaky breath. That was un-fucking-believable.

But before losing his fight with sleep, he realized neither of them had spoken a word.

CHAPTER 5

THE SUN WARMED HER CHEEK. Why would she have fallen asleep naked in the park with her dog?

Colby cracked her eyes open and found herself blinded for a second. Her childhood dog didn't lie next to her. No. Mace did. She was on his bed, not in a park. But she certainly was naked. No doubt about that.

An equally naked, but hairy, leg trapped her thigh and a heavy arm crossed her chest, pinning her to the bed. And one hand cupped her breast possessively. Sneaking a peek at Mace, she breathed a sigh of relief when she realized he still slept, his breath softly escaping his parted lips in a steady rhythm.

She had made a big—*no, no, no, huge*—mistake letting her emotions—more like her hormones—get away from her and sleeping with a man she only knew for three days. Okay, four now. Even so, she hardly knew him.

She had promised herself she wouldn't get into this type of situation again. Never again. But here she was…

Dumb, dumb, dumb.

She slowly eased out from under his arm. They both needed to forget about last night. She wasn't ready to get involved with this man, or any other.

She needed to escape his room before he woke. As she slipped from his hold, she smothered a groan. A little stiff and sore, she used muscles last night she had forgotten about or never knew she had. Just thinking about some of the moves they did made her body react all over again.

Then she spotted the clock, and her heart stopped. 8:28!

Shit! She had to be at work at nine. Not only did she have to shower and dress yet, it was a twenty-five-minute drive to get to campus.

Unable to drag the sheet along with her without waking Mace up, she rushed down the hall with only her pile of clothes pressed to her chest. Once in the bathroom, she locked the door behind her and jumped into the shower.

Her hair still damp, she pulled on her work clothes in a rush. With one shoe on, she attempted to slip on the other while racing down the hall, only to stop short at the sight of Mace leaning against the wall next to the stairwell.

Wearing only his shorts, his bare chest made her breath catch. Were those teeth marks near his nipple? Damn, she remembered biting and licking and flicking her tongue along those tight, hard nubs.

"Mace..." She cursed herself for sounding so breathless. Of course, it was because she was in a hurry and had nothing to do with the sight of his muscular pecs. *Yeah, right.*

"Late?" he asked with a cocked brow, like he had nothing better to do than to watch her rush around like a fool.

"More than late." She finally got the troublesome shoe on her foot. When she straightened, she avoided his eyes. And everything else.

"I wanted to thank you—"

She started down the steps, tucking her blouse into her slacks. "Not now, we'll talk later."

She didn't mean to blow him off, but she had no time to chat if she wanted to keep her damn job. And she desperately needed it. Plus, she didn't want to rehash what happened. Not now. Hurrying through the foyer, she snatched her briefcase.

"I'll make dinner," he called down the steps. "What time do you get off work?"

"Five." She slammed the front door behind her. Standing on the stoop, she realized she forgot her car keys.

The front door cracked open, and Mace's arm reached out, her key-ring jingling on the tip of his finger. "I'll have dinner at six. Don't forget."

Colby snagged the keys and raced to her car, calling, "Okay! I'll be there."

THE SCENT of dinner immediately struck Colby when she opened the door. She was so freaking late. Not used to having someone waiting for her at home anymore, she hadn't even thought to call the house. But, honestly, she didn't realize he'd been serious when he said he would make dinner.

After setting her briefcase on the foyer table, she kicked off her shoes to pad quietly down the hall to the kitchen.

If he was angry, he had every right to be. *Damn.* She screwed up again. Unfortunately, it was becoming her life story.

She peered around the doorway and saw the table set, the glasses filled with what looked like red wine and Mace nowhere in sight. The coast looked clear. For now.

Colby stepped cautiously into the kitchen. Pots filled the sink, and a cookbook lay open on the counter. "Mace?"

Silence.

She compared her watch to the clock on the wall to make sure it was correct. It was. 8:15.

"Damn, I'm so sorry," she whispered to the empty room.

"Not a problem," came the deep voice behind her.

Colby jumped, her heart stopping for an instant. She spun to face him, hoping he would understand, hoping...just hoping she hadn't hurt him by standing him up. "Mace, I'm so sorry."

He lazily lifted one shoulder. "You already apologized."

"I should have called. I just didn't think. I'm not used to coming home to—"

"No big deal," he cut her off as he brushed past her. When he reached the sink, he turned to face her. "Really."

She swept her arm toward the table, indicating the place settings and the now cold candle stubs. They must have burned for a while; wax had dripped all over the tablecloth.

She couldn't meet his eyes, though he didn't seem angry, or hurt, but... "No, it *was* a big deal. I didn't realize you would make a big meal. More than just spaghetti."

"I did."

"What?"

Her gaze flicked to his face, but he abruptly turned to the sink and began to scrub the pots, putting a little more effort into it than necessary. "I made spaghetti. Whole wheat, by the way. With a white clam sauce and cheesy garlic bread. I kept some warm for you. Want it?"

"Do...Do you want me to have some?" she asked carefully, trying to judge his mood.

He smacked a wet pot into the drain pan. "Of course. I made it for you, didn't I?" If he could make her feel any worse, he succeeded.

"Yes, I'd love some. But let me go change. I'd hate to get sauce all over my work clothes."

"I'll have it ready for when you come back down."

Colby raced up the stairs and changed in a flash. Dressed in a pair of khaki shorts and an old Elton John T-shirt, she hurried back downstairs.

Mace sat across from her while she ate. And she finished every last piece of spaghetti on her plate. She complimented his cooking between mouthfuls of delicious pasta. She smiled between bites and kept the little conversation they had as light as possible. His mood seemed to loosen a bit, the effect she strove for. But she had to admit, the meal tasted great. And he'd been thoughtful enough to make the garlic bread out of a whole grain loaf.

Before she could clear her own dishes, he brushed her hands away from her plate and had them washed, rinsed, and carefully placed in the drain pan.

He was wonderful.

Too wonderful. She kept waiting for the other shoe to drop since she wasn't used to this controlled anger. She hurt his feelings, and she swore to herself she wouldn't do it again.

Colby poured herself another glass of wine. Sipping at it, she waited for him to make the next move. She wished he would scream at her for being late or so callous for not calling. She wished he would yell at her for something. But he didn't.

She was used to men expressing themselves loudly. She didn't know how to deal with a man who brooded silently.

Maybe she was wrong. Maybe it hadn't been such a big deal after all. Maybe she only imagined the undercurrents between them. Maybe the unnecessary paranoia was all in her head...

Maybe.

MACE WATCHED Colby refill her wine glass for the third time and wondered if she truly regretted missing his—*their*—dinner. He normally didn't cook, but he wasn't telling her that. And she hadn't even seen the dessert he had stashed in the fridge yet. Yes, she apologized, but...

When he sat alone at the dinner table at six, at seven, then until eight, he realized Colby had better things to do with her life than come home to a cripple. They had no ties, just some casual sex. And even then, only once. The woman had her own life to live.

Most likely, she ate dinner before coming home. Maybe with her assistant Matt, or whatever his name was. She probably only ate his meal after seeing the table he had set and feeling sorry for him.

Fuck if he would let her know how it had affected him. It was easier to just blow it off and pretend it didn't.

Though she was downing the wine right now, and he wasn't sure what to make of it. One would think after their amazing sex session last night, she wouldn't need to get drunk to spend a little time with him. Maybe she had all day to think about how she didn't want to be with someone who was damaged goods.

The room had been dark last night; maybe she couldn't bear the thought of fucking him again in the light when she could see his shortcomings. *Whatever.* He was a big boy, he could get over it.

But when Colby suggested they go relax in the den, he picked up the half-empty wine bottle, grabbed his glass, and followed her. He stopped short in the doorway separating the kitchen from the den. What was he doing? Following her around like a lost, lonely puppy?

He was about to turn around and leave when Colby patted the couch next to her. He obediently sat, placing the bottle on the coffee table. Look what a little sex could do to him. Make him a pussy-whipped, pussified pussy.

And ripe for another letdown.

"So, how does your leg feel?"

Mace grimaced. His leg was the last thing he wanted to talk about. "A little stiff."

She turned toward him after putting down her glass. "Why?"

"I started physical therapy again this morning."

"Physical therapy? Where?"

Was she really interested? Or just trying to make small talk? "Community General."

"Will you go every day?"

"No. Three times a week, but I have to work out here at home every day."

"Is it painful? No, don't answer that, I know it has to be."

His fingers clenched around the stem of his wine glass. *Goddamn it.* He didn't want her sympathy. "I don't care. I want to walk. I want to be normal again. I don't want to walk with a cane or a walker like an old man. I don't want to be handicapped for the rest of my life. I need to redevelop my muscles as much as I can."

"You're not handicapped." She placed her warm fingers around his forearm.

He studied the contrast of her delicate, white hand next to his darker skin. He said, "No? I feel like it," with a little more force than was necessary. He shook his head and took a deep breath before continuing. "In my line of work, limping is a handicap."

"It's not so bad."

He laughed, though he couldn't keep the bitterness out. "I'm surprised you say that after you saw it last night."

Colby shrugged. "It doesn't bother me."

"Well, it bothers me."

She squeezed his arm slightly. "Mace—"

"Colby." He hesitated for a split second before the rest of the words escaped in a jumble. "Will you help me with my physical therapy?"

Damn. Even though he wanted her help, he didn't want to ask her like this. Not after the dinner fiasco. Fuck, now he'd just have to hope she'd say yes.

Her eyes widened, and her mouth dropped open before closing it to say, "I don't know. I don't know what to do."

Well, it wasn't a definite no. He figured working together would be good for her, for him. For them. He was just like her house: a work in progress, a project to tackle. "Come on, it's not hard. Look, the hospital is only a few miles from the University. Why don't you stop in on your lunch hour at my next session? My therapist would be glad to show you what to do."

He wanted—*needed*—her help. Hell, he wanted her in general. He needed to see her red hair spread over his pillow while he pounded her until she came. The small mewing sounds she made last night filled his head all over again. After wiggling into a more comfortable position for his growing cock, he blew out a long, slow breath, bringing his thoughts back to the topic at hand.

At her continued hesitation, he decided it was time to pull out all the stops. "I'll make you a deal. You help me out with my exercises, and I'll help you out with your house." He knew she couldn't resist that offer. His desire to walk normally was just as strong as her desire to finish her house. Whatever her reasoning. He raised his wineglass to her. "Deal?"

After a moment, her glass rang against his. "Deal."

He couldn't wipe the smile off his face.

CHAPTER 6

"YOU KNOW, tomorrow's Saturday, and there's a lot to be done at the house."

Mace lifted his head off the treatment table to see Colby beelining toward him. His heart thumped a little harder and a lot faster while he watched her slender figure work its way across the PT room. Relief at her actually showing up flooded through him.

Robin, his physical therapist, finished the set of exercises with him before asking, "Is this the woman you want me to teach?"

"Yep, that's her." He leaned over closer to his therapist and said in a stage whisper, "She's pretty smart, she should catch on quickly."

"Hey, I heard that!"

After Colby introduced herself to Robin, she shook hands with the older, heavyset woman and said, "From what I've seen so far, it doesn't look hard."

He caught the rush of color up her neck and over the freckles sprinkled across her nose. He pointed his gaze at Robin, who was about three times Colby's size and twenty years older, to keep from getting a huge hard-on.

"It's not. However, he should do a certain amount of exercises daily, and he needs help. It's not easy doing it alone," Robin admitted.

"He's an easy patient because he wants to get better, not like some others I've worked with. And if you forget anything, I'm sure he'll remember. He knows the routine. His previous therapist did a good job."

"You know, I'm still in the room here. I may be crippled, but I'm not deaf." Mace toweled the sweat off his brow. Some of it was from his PT and some...Well, he fought to keep his thoughts from the other night.

Robin leaned over him to say, "You need to put a dollar in the jar for using the 'C' word again." Luckily, the woman was all bark and no bite.

He chuckled. "Robin, explain the exercises to her while I take a break."

"No way, no how. I'll use you to demonstrate. Colby, will you grab the blue exercise band over there?"

Mace faked a groan though he really didn't mind the extra exercises. The more he did, the better he felt—until later, when it caught up with him. Colby watched Robin put him through his next set of stretches with the wide rubber band. At least concentrating on the exercises kept his thoughts clean.

For forty minutes, Robin explained and demonstrated different stretches and exercises. The therapist would switch places with her, making sure Colby knew how to assist Mace correctly.

In the end, sweat drenched him, and Colby looked like he felt. Tired.

Robin threw him a clean towel and left to grab a pad of paper to jot down notes for Colby. While she was gone, he took full advantage of their alone time.

He was raising himself up on his elbows when she said, "It's a lot to remember."

He wanted to erase the uncertainty from her expression, but he knew his PT could be daunting at first. "Between Robin's notes—and me—it won't be a problem. I know this is asking a lot of you."

"Don't be silly. I want to help." She gave him a tentative smile.

Then, she ran a hand down his arm and squeezed his fingers. The gesture reassured him.

"There will be other exercises we can do also, ones which won't be in Robin's notes."

"Oh, like what?" She glanced down at him, still lying on the table. A fraction of a second later, the blush returned in full force. "Oh."

"Those exercises are much more fun."

"I'll bet. Mace—"

He already figured she regretted that they fucked the other night. It was too obvious not to notice. Not to mention, she had avoided any intimate contact since. But he wouldn't give up on getting her beneath him again. Or on top. He wasn't choosy. He just wanted to feel her hot, wet, tight pussy sliding over his cock. Slow and teasing at first, then hard and fast until they were both desperate for release. He imagined their bodies connected, slapping together over and over until his balls tightened and convulsed and—

Shit.

Robin suddenly stood over him again. He quickly threw his damp towel over his lap. Colby's ears were purple from embarrassment. Christ, she must have been imagining it, too.

With a shaky hand against her throat, it took three attempts before she asked, "Is it really necessary for him to take those painkillers? Aren't they addictive? I would like to try some herbal remedies on him."

Those questions were enough to cool his wicked imagination. "You are not taking my pills away," he warned. He might want to fuck her until she screamed—hell, until he screamed—but he wouldn't tolerate her controlling his life. She was not his mother...or his wife.

"Mace, you can try natural stuff without getting rid of your Vicodin," Robin assured him. "And to answer your question, Colby, yes, any painkillers with hydrocodone can be addictive. But pain has a way of bringing someone's self-esteem down. We think it's more beneficial for healing if the patient feels better. Relieving or minimizing the pain does wonders for people. It rids them of the constant reminder they're ill or injured, and it gives their body a chance to really heal." Robin indicated to Colby they should switch places.

Robin continued, "But painkillers are his choice. You don't have to take them, Mace, you know that. Colby, if you can help him with herbs or whatever, more power to you. I like to keep things natural myself. But it has to be his decision. As long as you continue your rehab, Mace, that's the most important thing, redeveloping your muscle tone and keeping it flexible."

He lay back on the table and smiled. "I think I like having two women's hands all over me."

Robin rolled her eyes. "Take your pants off; it's time for your favorite part."

He grinned when Colby's face turned the same color as her hair once again.

COLBY DIDN'T NEED to look in a mirror to see she was beet-red. But she made a deal with Mace. More like a deal with the devil. He had kept up with his part so far, now she had to stick with hers.

He had helped her all day at her house, not complaining once. Well, maybe once.

But it wasn't like he hadn't kept up with kicking ass beside her. They accomplished more than she ever thought they would. They had pulled and scraped all the old wallpaper off the walls upstairs. She had hoped to get one bedroom stripped and prepared for paint. Amazingly, they ended up doing all four.

Now, she had to do the things Robin had taught her yesterday. Like it or not.

Even though they were both damp with perspiration, Mace's sweat stemmed more from pain than exertion. After working through his exercises using his bed as a make-shift PT table, they were now at his "favorite part." He'd shucked his sweats in anticipation and now lay on the sheets, wearing only his boxer briefs and a T-shirt.

As she leaned over the bed, Colby tried not to zero in on areas she needed to keep her eyes—and hands—off. But she needed to work close to the area her eyes kept flicking back to. And it wasn't as if Mace hadn't responded to her closeness.

She suddenly found it difficult to swallow since she noticed the long, hard line of his cock against the snug cotton.

"You don't have to do this, Colby. You worked hard all day, too. I'll understand if you don't want to."

Colby realized she was chewing on her lower lip and released it. "No. I...I'll do it. Robin said it would help relax the muscle and keep it from cramping."

"I don't know how my muscles will relax with your hands all over me."

Could her face get any hotter? "Not *all* over you."

"Well, if you're going to do it, do it. I feel—" Mace gave her an over-exaggerated frown. "Exposed. Like a sitting duck."

She laughed, suddenly a little more relieved. So, she wasn't the only one uncomfortable about this. In more ways than one. "Okay, tell me if I hurt you."

Holding her breath, she timidly placed her hands on the remains of his inner thigh muscle and massaged. Though she had no problems touching his body the other night, it seemed different tonight. She felt different. She was beginning to really...*like* the man, instead of just lusting after him.

She enjoyed his company and his sense of humor. His shadow of a beard and long, dark brown hair were not only sexy, but reminded her of a renegade. A loose cannon. Completely opposite to her staid, boring scientist self.

She needed to loosen up. Ever since that dark night Mace Walker crept into her life, she noticed she felt a little freer, a bit more content. Maybe it was just her imagination, but those multiple orgasms the other night had released something in her, something she didn't want to admit—

Mace groaned. She glanced down; her hands were way too high, too close to his hard-on. She pulled away in dismay. "I'm sorry, I didn't mean to hurt you."

"You didn't. It feels good. You were massaging so...intently."

He caught her hands in his, which emphasized how much smaller she was than him. They were half his size. Colby remembered how those thick, masculine fingers felt dipping into her, strumming her, making her body tremble and writhe in pleasure. She pressed her lips together to capture her groan.

After bringing her hands back to his thigh, he squeezed slightly before releasing them. "Keep going."

She did so, but more tentatively, paying more attention to what she was doing.

"What were you thinking about?"

"What?" Colby glanced up to see his dark eyes attempting to peer into her soul. His heated stare burned her, leaving a sensation of hot liquid flowing down her spine to her toes. Her knees wobbled, and her words caught in her throat. "Work." She tried again, "I was thinking of work. Martin and I are close to completing a project."

The spark in his eyes suddenly flickered and died. He must find her work uninteresting.

"Do you and Marty work closely together a lot?"

His muscle tightened, so she kneaded a little faster. "His name is Martin and, yes, we always work together. I told you, he's my assistant."

His eyes narrowed. "That's about all you told me. Do you work late on projects together a lot? Like the other night, I mean."

She kept her rhythm going even though her fingers were tiring. Not to mention, the topic of work cooled the heat between her legs. "Not usually. We try not to do too much overtime. First of all, we're both salaried and second, we don't want to burn out."

"Yeah, you need to keep your energy level high for those special projects. Is that right?"

His hostile tone caught her off guard. Once again.

She stopped massaging his leg and stepped back from his bed. "I don't know what you're insinuating. But if you're accusing me of something...Do you think...I...We..." She picked up his sweat pants off the floor and whipped them into his lap, frowning. "I think you need a shower. You stink!"

As she turned to leave, Mace caught her arm, spinning her back toward him. "Colby."

He looked apologetic, but she didn't care. She ripped her arm from his grasp. "No, Mace. I think I understand now. Perfectly. Even if Martin and I are having a relationship or whatever..." She stabbed her finger into his chest. "It's..." Poke. "None..." Poke. "Of..." Poke. "Your..." Poke. "Damn business."

After a few more jabs for good measure, she stormed out of his room and down the hall, leaving Mace rubbing his chest.

She slammed her bedroom door and asked it, "Who the hell does he think he is?" The door didn't answer her.

77

CHAPTER 7

"You know, our deal was we would help each other out."

Colby dropped the paintbrush, watching in dismay as it sank like an ocean liner into the can of forest green paint. She muttered a curse and picked up a paint stirrer which she used to try to fish the brush out. Unsuccessfully.

"Here. Let me help you."

He had the nerve to stand there, handsome and sexy in a snug black T-shirt, while his dark eyes pleaded with her to forgive him. She pushed his hand away. "No thanks."

"Are you still mad at me?"

His low voice caused tingling sensations down her spine. She would *not* feel bad for being angry with him. Nope. "Why would you think I was mad?"

Mace pulled his shirt up and showed her the small purple bruise on his chest. "Oh, I don't know, maybe I had a good reason."

Okay, now she felt awful. As much as she didn't want to, she did. She was supposed to help him with his rehab, not injure him.

"I'm sorry for being a jerk last night. You're right; it's none of my business. Your life is your own."

"Yes." She gave up on the lost brush and searched for a new one.

"Yes?" He watched her in confusion.

"Yes, you were a jerk. Yes, it's none of your business. Yes, it's my life."

Mace smiled and gave her a sideways glance. "Do you forgive me?" He found another brush before she did and picked it up. After dropping on one knee, he brandished the brush like a jeweled sword, a peace offering for a princess. "My Lady, if I finish painting thy wicker furniture this lovely shade of green, will you forgive me? Or will it be off with my head?"

Colby studied him for a moment, wondering if she should let him off the hook. After all, he let her off the hook the other night when she missed dinner. Eventually.

She glanced at all the pieces of wicker furniture which had been delivered earlier from the secondhand shop in town. They littered the living room. She wanted to get them painted so as soon as the porch was finished, she could put them outside. "I'll think about it. Maybe if the coats are even and there aren't any runs."

"You're tough."

She was, and she'd be the first to admit it. Not out loud, though. But she had to be. She wouldn't let this man walk into her life and turn it upside down and inside out. She'd been in a relationship like that before and ended up on the losing end. She wasn't going get burned ever again. Even if it meant she might never find someone permanently. One of those "forever" type of men. She'd rather be alone for the rest of her life than go through that humiliation and pain again.

When she'd been lucky enough to secure her position at Malvern U, the move here had given her a fresh start and put a good distance between her and her ex-boyfriend Craig—a mean, controlling bastard. She couldn't believe she wasted two years with him. Two years!

That final time in the hospital made her wake up. She was tired of taking the blame for things she didn't do. The day she walked out of the hospital, she walked out on Craig. With a restraining order in hand, she boarded a bus and headed toward Malvern. That had been over a year ago. She was sure he was too busy with his new girlfriend —the one he had been fucking while living with, and supposedly in love with, Colby—to care she had disappeared.

The more she thought about it, the more foolish she felt. She swept the memories out of her head like cobwebs.

As Colby watched Mace paint the chairs, she thought she could always get a dog to keep her company. A dog would be more faithful and love unconditionally. A dog wouldn't cheat on her. At least, she hoped not.

"Hellooooo?"

She shook her head, clearing her thoughts. "What?"

"I just asked you where you're going to put this furniture three times. If you haven't decided yet, I suggest the porch. After it's safe, of course."

"The porch is exactly where it will go. The contractor said it should be completely repaired and ready for paint by the end of the month."

"Dare I ask what color? Or is it going to be an awful shade of pink?"

"No one calls pink 'pink' anymore. It's either rose or blush, jeez," she teased. "But no, it's going to be cream." She smirked at the relief he didn't bother to hide. "I've decided to paint the exterior of the house cream and accent it with this forest green. And maybe some gold." She brushed a piece of flyaway hair, an escapee from her braid, away from her face. "Or possibly red."

"Not sunshine yellow like in the kitchen?"

"You hate that color, don't you? But I wanted something bright and sunny for the best and most used room in the house. It's the center of a home, people gather there. It's where people chat and enjoy meals together or a late cup of hot cocoa on a cold winter night."

"I prefer to have something hot late at night in bed. But the kitchen table would do."

Typical man with only one thing on his mind. But after he said it, she couldn't shake the thought of having sex with Mace on the kitchen table. Would it be uncomfortable? It was something she'd never tried before and might be a great prop—

Colby jumped when he placed his hands on her shoulders. He leaned in close to her, murmuring in her ear, "Are you thinking what I'm thinking?"

His breath stirred the loose hair by her ear, tickling her, sending a shiver up her spine. Her nipples hardened, and her pussy squeezed in anticipation. His lips were close enough that if she tilted her head just slightly...

She shook it instead. "Only if you're thinking how perfect this furniture will look on the porch."

Mace ran his hands down her arms and took the paintbrush from her fingers. After placing it on a lid, he turned her to face him. His large, warm hands cupped her cheeks. "I have fantasies of taking you on these drop cloths. In some of them, I paint designs all over your body, slowly swirling the brush in sensitive places, like your lips, your breasts, your—"

"Mace." Her heart skipped, and a split second later, resumed beating violently. Warmth rushed between her legs, making her panties hot and damp. She needed him to touch her. She wanted his lips against hers, so male, so warm. Before she changed her mind, she pulled his head down to capture his mouth, smothering his sound of surprise.

He gripped the small of her back to press her against him. She couldn't be more aware of his body, his desire clearly matching hers. She couldn't deny how much she wanted him, especially when her body gave her away.

Trembling, she yanked the T-shirt from his jeans and slid her hands beneath the thin cotton, running them over the scorching heat of his chest. Her fingers followed the contours until she reached his small male nipples, her thumbs circling the tight nubs. The desire to rake her teeth against them overcame her; she wanted to hear a quick intake of breath when she nipped his skin. Maybe leave another love bite.

"This isn't fair; I should be doing this to you. Take it off," he ordered, his voice so gruff, it sounded nearly painful.

She didn't hesitate to tear his shirt over his head and toss it aside. All the exercises he did kept his muscles hard and lean. Just to see them excited her; except now, she got to touch them, experience the searing smoothness of his skin, the roughness of the dark hair disappearing into his waistband.

He fingered the button on his jeans.

"No." Colby stopped him, brushing his hands away. "Let me."

He dropped his arms to his side, and his eyes became dark, clouded, as she released the top button and slowly slid the zipper down.

Mace growled softly when the back of her knuckles grazed his hard length. "Fuck. You're going to kill me." He grabbed her by the back of her arms and pulled her against him. "At least," he murmured against her lips, "I'll go with a smile."

He lowered her down to the drop cloth, slowly following her, and unbuttoned the baggy work-shirt hiding her curves.

Colby closed her eyes for a moment as the air cooled her hot skin. She opened them when he released the clasp of her bra and then pulled it and her shirt off her arms. Mace knelt over her, staring at her breasts.

Then he grasped both of them with his hands and softly kissed each nipple. She arched her back, thrusting herself closer to his mouth, his lips, his tongue.

"So beautiful. You shouldn't be allowed to wear clothes."

His words made Colby shake her head in disbelief. She wondered how the University would react if she did lab work naked.

"No, forget that. I want no one to see you naked except me. I want to see every inch of you, every nook, every cranny."

She shivered and became lost once again.

He buried his face between her breasts, murmuring, "Colby, stop me now if you have any doubts."

She swept her tongue over her lips and whispered, "Mace, please..."

He paused.

"Touch me."

Then his body molded against hers as he nuzzled her neck and nibbled her earlobe. Stroking the outer shell of her ear with his tongue, he murmured naughty ideas, making her head spin.

And she wanted to try every one of them.

He captured her lower lip between his teeth, tugging slightly, before kissing each corner of her lips. "Sweet...so sweet. I want to taste you everywhere."

He released the buttons on her jeans, shucking them and her panties off with a practiced move. They were tossed into a corner, quickly followed by his own.

"Done that much?"

He stopped her words with his mouth, their tongues sparring fiercely. Colby's nails dug into the skin of his back, while her hips danced against his. His cock, the head slick with precum, felt like hard steel encased in satin. She quickly forgot what she asked when his cock bumped, slid and bumped again against her hip. Her pussy opened wider, became wetter.

The roughness of his thumb stroking her nipple was enough to make her clench her thighs together to keep control. He pinched and plucked one, then the other, making her cry out. She pressed her lips against his throat and couldn't stop herself—she sank her teeth into the corded muscles. His neck bowed, and he threw his head back, groaning. Then he shifted until his very ready cock was between her thighs, teasing, sliding against her swollen clit.

Before Mace, it had been a long time since she actually enjoyed sex, and she was determined to get pleasure from every second of it with him. She would take as much as he wanted to give. But she wanted to give back too, to savor every inch, every hard curve and every tight line of his body. She wouldn't ignore those soft places either.

One hand left her breast and brushed against her wet curls—a slight brush that almost made her come. She ran her tongue over the teeth marks she left on his throat, and with a curse, he shoved two fingers deep within her, circling his thumb against her clit. Her back arched, and she cried out his name.

With a stroke to her swollen lips, she opened to him. And fingers were no longer enough; she needed more. "Fuck me," she begged in a tortured moan. "Now. *Please.*"

He pinched her nipple harder and pulled out his slick fingers only to clench his fist around her braid, forcing her head back, exposing her vulnerable throat.

He licked along the hollow of her neck before leaning back to ask, "Are you ready?"

His grimace showed his fight for control, but he teased her. Teased her!

"Damn you!"

He still held back, his cock sliding along her thigh, twitching against her skin. "I want to make sure you're ready."

She reached down, grabbed his cock and drew him to her slick opening. She bared her teeth at him and demanded, "Now."

From where he got it, she didn't know, didn't care, but he held up a condom and waved it in front of her face.

"Need something?" he teased.

She ripped the foil package out of his hand, tore it open with her teeth, and without even a hesitation, rolled it over his shaft, lingering for only a fraction of a second. She didn't want his cock in her hand, she wanted it elsewhere.

After scooting back onto the drop cloth, she bent her knees and spread her thighs in anticipation as he settled between them. Between their bodies, she saw the head of his cock right there, against her opening, ready to take her.

She glanced up, wondering why he waited. Once she looked at

him and their gazes held, he drove deep with a sharp tilt of his hips. Once. She waited for the second thrust.

When it didn't come, she writhed and cried out, begging, but he refused to move. He stilled, buried deep within her. He sucked oxygen in a clear struggle to keep himself together.

However, only seconds ticked by before he relented and met every thrust of her hips with one of his own—over and over until he could bury himself no deeper. She dug her fingers into his ass, controlling his thrust, controlling the angle of his hips. When he brushed her sweet spot, she closed her eyes and screamed. Her climax pulsated from the center and exploded outward, and, within seconds, he joined her on the other side, his arms shaking and his body curving like an archer's bow.

They were aware of nothing but each other, the resulting pain and pleasure. Colby closed her eyes, a shaky sigh escaping her. "Oh, my God," she whispered.

"I think I saw him, too."

Her eyes opened at his husky words, and she blinked to focus on him directly above her. He gave her a crooked smile before pushing himself up to relieve her of some of his weight.

She frantically grabbed his arm. "No, don't go."

"I'm not going anywhere, Colby. I'm exactly where I want to be. But I don't want to crush you."

Mace shifted onto his side beside her, breaking their intimate contact. She stretched leisurely, savoring the tightness of her hard-worked muscles and the dampness between her legs.

He caressed her braid and drew circles around her navel with the end of it. "It's a mess."

He tugged gently on it. "Next time, I want your hair loose so I can bury my hands in it. I want to feel the soft, silkiness against my skin. I want—"

"What about what I want?"

He propped his head in his hand and searched her face a moment before giving her a wide smile. "I'll give you anything you want, everything you need."

She trailed a finger down his damp chest, following the dark line of hair circling his navel. Then she reached up and undid her braid, slowly freeing the long, silky strands.

When she finished, she said to him in a husky voice, "I want you again. Now."

His smile turned into a wicked grin. "I'll do my best to comply."

He pushed himself to his feet, and without a care, he went into the kitchen to dispose of the condom. When he returned, he paused in the doorway, clearly not ready for a second round.

Colby raised an eyebrow and gave him a meaningful look.

"Don't worry. It won't take me long."

"Promises, promises."

"Believe me. I have plans, and I came prepared."

Apparently. Because after finding where his jeans landed earlier in his haste, he pulled a fresh condom and a small tube of something out of the pocket, and slowly approached the drop cloth where she still lazed. Even tired and boneless, she had an itch deep inside her only he could scratch. Magnificent when naked, his only flaw was his injury, and even that didn't take anything away from him.

"Are you okay?" She eyed the tube which he had tossed to the side when he dropped to his knees. She was now curious about why he'd need that or what his "plans" were.

"I'm fine," he responded. Though he probably wouldn't admit if he wasn't, she wouldn't push it.

She crooked a knee up, breaking his view of her most intimate parts. He came over and settled on his knees between her legs. Putting a hand on each knee, he spread them apart. "Don't hide yourself."

"I wasn't."

He only shot her a look. He ran a finger up both sides of her inner thighs until they met in the middle, then slid his palms around to her

JEANNE ST. JAMES

hips. "Flip over." He helped her turn over until she laid on her stomach, legs spread.

She didn't need to see what he was doing; she just wanted to enjoy his touch. Lips brushed along the back of her knees up to the tops of her thighs. Teeth and tongue scraped along her ass cheeks, making her flex her muscles there. She heard his deep chuckle behind her. "Jesus, your ass is so sweet." He palmed her cheeks and squeezed them together, the sensation making her even wetter.

Colby finally turned to peek at him when he yanked her hips up and back, leaving nothing of her to his imagination. He held her hips in place and just stared. And stared...until she became paranoid. Was something wrong with her?

She tried to wiggle away, but he gripped her harder. "Uh-uh." He was no longer semi-erect. He released one hip just long enough to roll on a condom. "Keep your head down and point your pussy toward the ceiling."

She tucked her head in her arms and bit her lip. She wanted him inside her already. What was he waiting for? "Are you going to fuck me or not?"

"Quiet."

She smiled at his short answer. Then he pushed against her inner thighs, spreading her a little bit more. Still nothing. She released a long, frustrated breath, trying to keep the whimper from escaping her. If he didn't fuck her soon, she would come just from anticipation!

When he slid between her ass cheeks, all the way up until his balls pressed against her pussy lips, she could no longer hold back the whimper. He did it again—pulled back and then slid between her crease, pushing her buttocks together as he did. Though it was a sensation she never experienced before, him sliding across that forbidden place, it felt so good. But she would never, could never do that.

He slid over her again, her ass cheeks still pinned together, and he let out an explosive breath mixed with a curse. He released one cheek just long enough to plunge two fingers into her wet pussy, and before she could even fathom what happened, he pressed his now slick fingers to her anus, rubbing the natural lubricant over it, circling her tight hole with his large fingers.

She whimpered again, from fear, from anticipation, from want.

No. She couldn't.

"It would be mine and mine only," he said as if he could read her mind.

Closing her eyes, she bit her bottom lip harder. He started a rhythm again with his cock, sliding between her cheeks, brushing against her. And every pass he took, she relaxed a little more, loosening, wanting.

He stroked his tongue up her spine, making her shiver. "Do you want me?"

"Yes."

"Do you want me inside you?"

"Yes."

"How badly?"

"I—"

"I will start in one and finish in the other."

No. No. Ahhh.

He plunged his cock into her pussy, slamming his hips against her. Again and again, hard, deep, and she loved it. She could come just like that, but he changed his position, bending over her back, keeping his cock fully seated, while he reached around and grabbed her breasts.

With his shallow movements inside her, she came. He pinched her nipples, and she screamed, bucking against him, wanting him to fuck her even harder. But he was relentless, continuing the grinding movements deep within her. Rubbing her nipples, pinching, and just when she thought her orgasm was over, it wasn't. She convulsed around him again, squeezing his cock. He would last longer this time, but she might just die of pleasure before he finished.

With a kiss to the back of her neck, he raised himself back up and took long strokes, reaching beneath her to circle her clit with his thumb. Again, she bucked wildly against him, but he wouldn't stop. His other thumb ended up at her rear entrance, stroking with the same rhythm as the one at her clit.

A low, tortured moan escaped her. The thumb at her tight ring circled, circled, pressing harder and harder. His cock slid out of her, and he returned to sliding it between her cheeks—slow, careful strokes. His other thumb still played with her clit. He adjusted himself again behind her, and two fingers filled her pussy, keeping in time with the thrusts of his cock.

Colby rocked back and forth on her knees, her head still tucked in her arms on the floor. She knew what came next. *She knew.* But she didn't even want to stop him.

Though he did. Just for a moment. Now she knew what the lube was for.

When he pulled back his hips to ready for another stroke, a slick finger slipped into her tight ring. She cried out and shuddered.

Mace tensed behind her, stopping his movement. A shudder ran through him as well. "Holy shit, you're so tight. Are you going to let me in?"

Was she? She nodded against her arms.

"Colby…" He sounded as if he were in pain.

She couldn't look at him, she couldn't. Her heart was going to burst. "Yes! Yes! Do it!"

He slipped his finger back out, creating the strangest feeling. And before she could suck in another breath, the head of his cock was there, pressing…slowly pushing, almost asking for permission from her body to enter. His command of "relax" sounded like it came from between gritted teeth. The cool sensation of lube being liberally applied against her heated skin made her jump.

But even so, she tried to relax, and when he stroked the insides of her pussy again with his fingers, she did automatically. The crown of his head broke through, and he slid slowly into her, stretching her, filling her.

His breathing became ragged and a drip of sweat fell onto the small of her back. For a fraction of a moment, he was fully seated inside her, his whole length deep within her. Then he gradually retreated, making her cry out.

"Are you hurting?"

"No...Fuck me." It felt strange and new, but...good. He picked up a gentle pace. Knowing he wouldn't go any faster drove her crazy. One of his hands controlled her, stopped her from impaling herself on him, while the other continued to fuck her pussy.

The buildup was slow this time—slow, but so intense, she screamed and tensed her whole body, tightening up on him. He took one more thrust, calling out her name as he spilled inside her.

He held her hips still until he recovered, then helped her down to the drop cloth as his cock slipped out of her.

Collapsing beside her, he took her into his arms and turned her to face him. He brushed a light kiss over her nose and sighed. "Tired?"

Colby could only nod slightly while she mentally did a body check.

"That was unbelievable." He flopped onto his back and dragged her over his chest.

She tasted the saltiness of his skin, then rolled her eyes up to see him staring intently at her.

"Are you okay?"

She gave him a smile. More than okay. "Perfect."

CHAPTER 8

A SHRILL RING jerked Colby awake. At the second ring, her heart pounded fiercely. She blinked, staring at where the old house phone sat on the nightstand.

It could be the person who kept hanging up. Or it could be Mace.

Even though she knew the phone would ring again, she still started when it did. She blew out a long breath, trying to calm her nerves. Until a second later when the doorbell rang.

She let out a little squeak.

She had to stop jumping at every little thing!

When Mace was home, she never worried. She felt safe whenever he was around, which surprised her since her first impression of him was he appeared dangerous.

Dangerous to whom? The jury was still out on that one.

After rolling out of bed, she grabbed the silk robe that hung on the back of the bedroom door. She slipped it on and tied the belt tightly around her waist, trying to ignore the still ringing phone. Someone must have switched off the answering machine. It could have been her, but she couldn't remember. It didn't matter at this moment anyway because someone was still ringing the doorbell. *Damn.*

She yanked open the nightstand drawer and grabbed her Glock, which was ready to go with one in the chamber and a full clip. But, looking down at her robe, she had nowhere to hide it on her person.

Hidden or not, she would not answer the door without protection. It could be anyone lurking outside the house. She shook her head; she was going loony. And was way too paranoid. But as she went downstairs, the feel of her heavy gun in her hand soothed her, made her not feel like a victim.

At the front door, she peered through the peephole. A young man stood on the other side, dressed in a brown uniform. His baseball cap had a patch sewn on it advertising *Ellie's Bouquets.*

Behind the kid, she noticed the business name plastered all over the parked delivery van as well.

Mace. He must have bought her flowers. Her heart fluttered at the sweet gesture.

After unlocking the door, she swung it partially open, just enough where she could keep her hand holding the gun hidden behind the door.

"Hello, ma'am," the kid said. He shoved his clipboard toward her. "I have a flower delivery."

The young man's eyes immediately drew to her cleavage where her robe gaped open. *Damn.* With the clipboard in one hand and the gun in the other, she had none left to close it.

"Who are they for?" Colby asked while she used the doorjamb to hold the clipboard and awkwardly signed on the line next to the address of the house. She handed it back to him before pinning the lapels of her robe together tightly with her free hand.

The kid did a lazy half-shrug, his eyes still focused on the point where she gripped her robe. "There's no name on the slip, just this address."

Colby looked down. Nope, nothing showed.

She waited as he stood, continuing to stare with a dumb look on his face, like he hoped to catch a glimpse of something.

She cleared her throat, catching his attention, and finally, his eyes. "The flowers?"

"Oh. Yeah. Here." He shoved the wrapped bouquet at her.

She had to quickly release her robe to grab the flowers, but then she pressed them against her chest, shielding herself.

He stood there for a moment more—until he got sick of waiting for a tip, she guessed. Not that he would get one from her since she didn't carry money in her negligee or robe, of course.

"Sorry," she called out as he trooped away mumbling.

She closed the door and locked it before heading into the kitchen where she dumped her gun on the table and quickly unwrapped the green paper covering the bouquet. A little thrill ran through her. She couldn't believe Mace bought her flowers!

As she peeled the paper away, she uncovered beautiful blood-red roses that smelled heavenly. She loved roses: the feel, the scent, the soft, silkiness of their petals.

Wait. What?

At first, Colby thought she was seeing things. She wasn't. In the center of the dozen red roses, a single deep purplish-black rose stood out. Though just as gorgeous as the red ones, the black color meant death.

Why would Mace include a black one? Maybe it was a simple mistake made at the florists. She laid the bouquet on the table and dug out the attached card. It read: *Thinking about you.* Without a signature line.

Not thinking *of* you, but thinking about you. Odd. The card did not indicate who it was to or from. Not only was it a bit out of the ordinary, the single black rose mixed in was as well.

She heard the front door unlock and open. "Mace?"

"Yeah?"

"I'm in the kitchen."

"Good. Did you get coffee started? If not, I brought—" He stepped into the kitchen, his hands full of a pastry bag and a drink carrier holding two large disposable cups. "What's the matter?"

"They delivered the flowers."

"Uh. Okay." He dumped the food and drinks on the table, then placed a cup in front of her. "Chai tea."

She nodded her thanks.

He pulled out a chair and settled into it, stretching his leg out. Looking a bit pained, a white ring circled the press of his lips.

"Is your leg bothering you?"

He nodded, kneading his knuckles against his thigh. "A little bit."

It had to be more than a little bit. When he reached for his bottle of pain medication which sat in the middle of the kitchen table, she made a noise. His fingers curled into a fist, and he grimaced, but he left the pain pills alone. Not that she enjoyed his suffering. She didn't. She just didn't want to see him end up addicted to pain medication.

He moved away from the pill bottle and brushed his fingers over the petals of the roses instead. "So, what's up with the roses?"

"You tell me."

He pursed his lips, clearly fighting with himself whether he should take credit for the flowers or not. If he had to think about it that hard, he didn't buy them.

"If you didn't order them, who did?"

"What does the card say?"

She tossed the card at him.

He glanced at it and frowned. "That's weird," he said, after putting the card aside.

"My thoughts exactly."

"Could it be your Martin?"

Colby sighed. "He's not *my* Martin. Anyway, I doubt he'd send me flowers."

"Why?"

"He just wouldn't. Maybe this is some sort of joke."

"An expensive joke." He took a long swig of his coffee.

She wrapped her brain around a more puzzling thought. "Hold on. How do we even know these were meant for me? The delivery guy just said they were for this address. Maybe they were sent to you."

He choked and wiped his mouth with the back of his hand. "No one knows I'm home except for you and my boss."

"And your physical therapist."

"Yeah, but—" He pulled out his cell. "We can solve this easily enough. What was the name of the florist?"

She gave him the information, but there wasn't a phone number on the card, so he Googled it and pressed Send. But a few minutes later, he hung up.

"Well, that was pointless." His attempt to not sound frustrated didn't go unnoticed. He sank back in his chair, running a hand through his hair.

"Sounded like it." She popped the lid off her tea and sniffed at it. The soft aroma of spices tickled her nose. She took a tentative sip. It tasted sweet and creamy and oh-so-good. Maybe it would calm her nerves.

"Whoever bought the bouquet paid in cash. They have no record of who sent it and who the intended recipient was. *Fuck.*" He dragged his hand through his hair again.

She fought the temptation to smooth it down for him. "Hey, it's just flowers." Though she had this niggling feeling, there was more to it. The people who knew she stayed at this address were limited, and Mace could say the same.

"Look, no point in worrying about it, I guess." He didn't sound so convinced. He pushed the pastry bag toward her. "I brought breakfast. Croissants and a couple danishes."

She gave the bag of food a look of distaste. She didn't know if she could eat now.

What was once the pleasant scent of the roses, now turned her stomach.

CHAPTER 9

COLBY SPREAD her legs and slowed her breathing. Mace reached around her to steady her arms, leaning into her back. His breath tickled the hair by her ear. "Steady, steady. Okay, squeeze."

The gunshot made Colby flinch, but her shot hit dead-on.

"Ouch," he groaned, looking at the target. He pressed the button and the paper target glided toward them. "You were supposed to go for center mass."

She grinned. "Close enough. I got him where I want him."

He stuck his pinky through the hole in the silhouette and wiggled it. "Yeah, right in the crotch. Sorry, buddy, there'll be no more lil' baby targets running around. She just neutered you."

With a laugh, she said, "Put another one out there."

He clipped a new target on, then pressed the button to send it out into the range. "Okay, this time—"

"This time, I can do it myself."

He lifted his hands in surrender and backed off. "Fine. Whatever. I only want to help."

"Mace, I wouldn't own a gun without knowing how to shoot it."

She barely caught the roll of his eyes. "Do you know what this world is filled with? People who buy firearms and can't—"

Colby gave him a quick elbow to the stomach. "Don't group me with them."

"All right, show me what you can do, Miss Biochemist." He brushed a kiss along her temple before backing off.

"That's *Ms.* Biochemist to you." She flashed him a big smile before turning to concentrate on her target. Supporting her trigger hand, she carefully took aim. Inhale, exhale all the air; steady. She kept an even pressure on the trigger and squeezed. The sound of the shot made her flinch again, but when she opened her eyes, she'd hit her target square.

"Nice. I want to see that again. But faster. Who will give you time to aim and shoot? A bad guy," he pointed to the target, "will not wait around for you to shoot him. He's either going to be running at you, running away from you, or blowing your head off."

Colby smiled wickedly. "Shut up and put your ears back on." He slid his hearing protectors back in place as she raised her Glock again. She called the body parts off as she aimed. "Head...Heart... Lung...Trigger arm...Groin...Leg..." Every bullet met its mark, one after the other, in quick succession. When nothing remained of the target but a tattered piece of paper, she slipped the clip out and double-checked the empty chamber. "He isn't going anywhere," she stated.

"Damn right, he's not." He shook his head. "Okay, we don't need to waste any more time here at the range. Let's go home, you're getting me hard." He chuckled and removed his shooting glasses. "Hot damn. A woman who can shoot *and* who's good in bed. How lucky can I get?"

"Don't push that luck." Colby popped out her orange earplugs and put the gun away in its case. "Wait a minute, just good?"

He reached around her to snap the case shut, then snagged her wrists before she could pull away. He yanked her arms above her head, and with his hips, he maneuvered her against the concrete wall of the shooting booth, letting her feel how much he wanted her.

She glanced quickly at the opening of the booth. Anyone could pass by at any moment. "Mace, someone will see us."

"Maybe."

She should be worried about the chance of getting caught. He pinned her against the wall and thrust against her. But she wasn't. Instead, the possibility of someone seeing them excited her.

He nuzzled her neck before moving up to her ear, then whispered, "I could fuck you right here."

He kissed her, slanting his lips over hers and burying his tongue in her mouth. He tasted so good. He shifted both her wrists to one hand then drew his fingers over her breasts and brushed over her nipples.

"Are you still sore?" he asked against her lips, referring to her tender backside, a result from their afternoon delight at the house the day before.

"A little." Actually, more than a little, but it had been worth it. Though she suffered with a slight case of discord afterward. She told herself to just live for the moment, to just enjoy what Mace offered. Even if it only lasted for a short while.

The man in question didn't ask, but took it upon himself to pop open her jeans. He unzipped them completely, giving his hand enough room to plunge beneath her panties and explore her pussy. Colby gasped at the sudden invasion of his fingers but tilted her hips to give him better access.

He stroked and tweaked her, playing along her slick labia, inserting a couple fingers before moving on to her clit where he started the pattern over again. When she cried out, he placed his lips over hers and caught it, muffling it. He kissed her deeply while he played with her, breaking away only to say, "This is my thank you for yesterday."

Curling his fingers inside her, he found her sweet spot, taunting and teasing it. He added his thumb into the mix, pressing and flicking her clit until she could take no more. Thrusting her hips against his hand one last time, she gasped and groaned into his mouth as her body convulsed around his fingers. He only released her when she quieted.

He brushed a light kiss against her lips. "Damn, I'll have to thank you more often."

She pulled herself together while he gathered their equipment. It took her a few minutes to move away from the wall and stand on her own. She was sure she wore the dumbest smile on her face.

On their way out of the gun club, Colby said, "I've got to stop and check on the contractor, do you mind?"

Their feet crunched along the graveled lot, and she noted the cars parked around her. There were at least a dozen. How could they have gone undetected? Maybe they hadn't. She had been so caught up in the pleasure, there could have been a huge audience, and she wouldn't have even known. Or cared at that moment.

"No." He unlocked the truck and opened the door for her. "I want to meet him, anyway."

She shot him a funny look at the sudden testosterone surge. "What for?"

"Why not? I can't meet the man who's working on your house?"

She climbed into the passenger seat. "Well, I didn't think you were so interested in my house. I know how atrocious you think it is."

"Maybe I just want to meet my competition. I know how much a man with a paint brush excites you."

Only you.

She tried not to laugh out loud. Wait until he meets the contractor.

When they drove up to the house, a crew of men was busy at work on the porch.

Colby's eyes widened. She hardly waited for Mace to stop the truck before leaping out.

"Hey, wait a minute," he called out.

"My porch! They're working on my porch!" She shot him a smile through the windshield and laughed. She practically ran up to the front steps. The hammering sounded loud and glorious. She loved it. The sound of those busy hands made her happy.

"Hi, Ben!" she yelled over the racket.

The older man turned to give her a slight wave. "Hello, Ms. Parks. Things are going real good here."

Colby hopped in place and wrung her hands together. Then she did the happy dance. "I see! You've got almost all the floorboards replaced." She probably looked like a crazy loon, but she didn't care.

"Yep, soon you'll be able to paint."

Music to her ears. A loud groan came from behind her. But not to someone else's apparently.

"Did I hear the 'P' word again?"

She turned and trotted up to Mace. "Hurry up! Look how far they've gotten." She tugged hard on his arm.

He slowly trudged up the overgrown walkway in mock misery. "I see. That's nice."

She tugged harder, trying to get him to pick up the pace. "Ben, this is Mace Walker. Mace, this is Ben Fine. He's my contractor."

"Oh, hell, I just thought he was collecting scrap wood for his fireplace." Mace turned to eye up the gray-haired man. "Hello, Ben."

Deep creases surrounding Ben's eyes and mouth and his weathered skin came from age and years of working in the sun. She watched Mace's expression relax, almost as if relieved. Why he would find her contractor a threat was a mystery.

Mace extended his hand and the older man shook it firmly while returning his hello. "Is the bedroom finished yet?"

The hammering stopped dead, and the crew's heads—all five of them—spun in unison to stare at Colby. Her face burned hot, and she turned on Mace. "Stop it," she whispered fiercely.

"What? I was just asking a question." He smirked, draping an arm around her hips and drawing her against him.

Colby jerked away impatiently and decided to ignore him and his childishness. As she wandered around the outside of the raised porch, she eyed all the new repairs. The crew had replaced broken spindles and rotted posts. The floorboards would eventually all be new. The steps still needed repair, but it looked like they would be finished by the next day.

She hugged herself, hardly able to contain her delight at the progress, and thought about how it would look with a fresh coat of paint. And the new porch swing she wanted. Soon! Soon she'll be swinging on her own porch, with a glass of lemonade, reading a novel and listening to the birds chirping, and the—

A hand on her shoulder startled her. "Come back from wherever you are," came the low murmur next to her ear.

Colby blinked twice, coming back to reality, and turned to look at the man next to her. Where did he fit in the picture?

"Oh, I was just doing a little daydreaming."

Did he even fit into the picture?

"Yeah, I could see that. You went off to Never Never Land."

"Mace, you just don't understand. This house is everything to me. It *is* me."

He laid an arm around her shoulders and squeezed. "I believe it. Now, how soon do we need to paint?"

MACE WANDERED around the back of the old house. Colby was still talking excitedly to Ben in the front, so he decided to get a little work done. He borrowed a carpenter pencil and measuring tape from one of the men and snagged a scrap of paper out of his truck. He needed to measure the rear entryway to the kitchen since she wanted to order a new storm door.

As he climbed the two wooden steps to the small covered entrance, he paused. Something wasn't right. Instinctively, he froze, searching his surroundings. Muddy footprints came from the overgrown bushes to the left of the house. Not from the right where the driveway was. And the empty paint cans he had stacked in a corner of the porch were scattered. The knocked-over cans he could attribute to a curious, wild animal. Maybe a raccoon. But the footprints were definitely human. And fresh.

He'd ask the crew whether any of them had done some exploring of their own. But his instinct told him something was off.

He shook his head. Even though his instinct was kicking in, the simple answer could be a teenager looking for an empty house to party in.

Just like some kid prank calling the house.

He finally moved, opening the outer storm door to inspect the inner wooden door carefully. He checked the small rectangular windowpanes. One had obvious palm prints. Like someone had peered in the back door, searching for something or someone.

Teenager, crew member, or not, he had a bad feeling about this. But he wasn't going to jump the gun and tell Colby. He didn't want to frighten her without reason. He would just keep a close eye on her and her house.

COLBY GLANCED at her watch. 1:13 a.m. She never meant to stay this late at work. But she got involved in an experiment and wanted to finish it. She hated leaving ends untied. As it was, she wanted to make up time for leaving early last Monday to go with Mace to the shooting range.

Her keys jingled softly when she inserted them into the door and slowly turned the doorknob. She expected Mace went to bed a few hours ago, and she didn't want to wake him if he was asleep. The only light in the foyer came from one of those lighted plug-in scents she had stuck in one outlet. And that was hardly a glow.

She slid her hand along the wall by the door until she found the switch and flipped it. A small, surprised cry escaped her when she turned to find Mace sitting at the top of the stairs in only sweat pants. How long had he been sitting there?

Okay, there isn't a problem.

"I didn't mean to wake you. I was trying to be quiet. Sorry," she whispered, even though it wasn't necessary since it was only the two of them in the house.

She needed to ignore whatever problem he perceived. She reminded herself that she was an adult who had a job. And as such, she should be able to work late without feeling guilty.

After closing the front door behind her, she locked it and carefully put her briefcase on the foyer table. She slipped her feet out of her shoes and straightened up to face him. His narrowed eyes were dark. Colby cringed.

"I couldn't sleep."

Damn it, she didn't have to answer to anyone. "Oh, do you want some tea? I'm going to make myself a cup of chamomile."

Without waiting for his answer, she headed into the kitchen, listening for his bare feet to pad down the stairs. When she didn't hear him, she assumed he went back to bed.

She grabbed a mug and a box of herbal tea bags out of the cabinet. After putting the kettle on the stove, she turned to take a seat at the table. Mace was already there. Colby jumped, her hand clutching her chest. "Jesus, you scared me. I didn't hear you come in."

When her heartbeat slowed, she grabbed another mug and tea bag, placing it in front of him. Then she settled into a chair across from him, waiting for the water to boil.

Or the other shoe to drop.

But, there is no problem. None whatsoever.

"Do you know what time it is?" His voice sounded low and grumbly.

There is no problem.

"Yes, unfortunately, I do."

She pulled her hairpins out, letting her hair fall around her face and down her back. What a relief to release her hair out the braid after a long day. She combed her fingers through the thick mass, untangling some snagged strands. "I'm beat. And to think I have to get up in a few hours and do it all over again."

"Do what?" His eyes pinned hers, and she felt like a moth caught in a flame.

"Do what? Work, of course." She unbuttoned the top button of her blouse.

"You were working?"

Colby stood to get the whistling kettle, breaking his eye contact. *There is no problem.* She filled both of their mugs with the steaming water. "What else?"

"I don't know, why don't you tell me?"

She put the kettle back on the stove and turned to him. *Okay, there may be a problem.* "Mace, what are you getting at?"

"I was just a little worried about you."

"Why? I'm a big girl."

"It was getting late, or should I say early. I thought you normally didn't work this late."

She stirred a little honey into her tea. "I don't. But, Martin and I—"

"Martin!" he spat.

Colby shot him an incredulous look. *There definitely is a problem.* "Yes, *Martin.* We got involved in a project we're working on, and before we knew it, it was late. At that point, we grabbed a late supper and—"

He held his hand up. "Enough. I've heard enough. You don't have to explain."

She slammed her spoon down on the table. *You better believe there's a problem!*

"You're damn right, I don't!" She stood, pushing her chair back. "I'm going to bed."

She bolted out of the room, trying not to spill her tea. As she carried it upstairs, she could have sworn she heard, "Been there, done that."

She slammed then locked her bedroom door, trying not to scream. Instead, she settled for some quiet fuming. In her head, she called him every name in the book. Who did he think he was? Just because they slept with each other, did he think he now owned her? No. She had already had someone who thought he owned her body and soul—and everything else. Look where it left her. She didn't need another man treating her like that.

She sat on her bed, sipping her tea but not enjoying it. There wasn't enough chamomile in the world to calm her down right now. Her doorknob slowly turned. She grinned smugly toward the door. She expected him to knock and apologize, but the doorknob released, and she heard nothing else.

Good. Let him go to bed by himself.

Though, if he hadn't acted like such an ass, she could have used the company. And everything that would have gone along with that.

THE NEXT MORNING came too soon for Colby. Still exhausted after barely three hours of sleep, she'd be lucky to function at work.

After showering, she crept downstairs, trying to avoid running into Mace. She decided to skip breakfast, instead grabbing her car keys and her briefcase as she snuck out the door undetected.

Unfortunately, her smooth escape came to a quick halt when her convertible wouldn't start. After pumping the gas pedal over and over, she finally gave up. Fighting back stinging tears, she rested her forehead on the steering wheel. She'd just had the water pump fixed, and she couldn't keep putting money into this car; she needed the funds for her house.

A tap on her window made her look up. *Mace.* She groaned. The last thing she wanted to do was face him this morning.

"Car problems?"

"It won't start."

"Pop the hood." After she did so, he lifted the hood and peered into the engine compartment. A few seconds later, he said, "Why don't you call in sick, and I'll check it out for you today."

Colby's eyes narrowed. "I don't call in sick."

He peered around the open hood. "Today, you will. In fact, I'll do it for you."

"No. I'm in the midst of a special project. I'll get a ride."

"Who? Marty?"

Mace had told her he knew about cars. He could have done something so her car wouldn't start. Would he do something so sneaky just to keep her away from Martin?

"Yes," she said, glancing at her watch. "I can probably catch him before he leaves." She climbed out of the little sports car.

If he wanted to play games, so would she. She knew Martin had most likely left for work by now. His drive to work took a lot longer than hers. But she wasn't telling him that.

When Mace cursed, she suspected her suspicions were correct.

"Don't bother. Here." He tossed his truck keys to her. "Don't wreck it."

Colby caught the keys and quickly turned away from him to hide her smile. "Thanks." She jumped in his truck and left before he had the chance to change his mind.

MACE KNEW how to become almost anyone. He could blend in anywhere, and he could sweet talk a woman into doing just about anything. Though, he was finding Colby a challenge. Not that he intended to give up any time soon.

Unfortunately, his plan this morning backfired. He had desperately wanted her to stay home with him, especially after getting screwed out of his time with her last night.

However, he hadn't expected her to hitch a ride with Martin. After she drove away in his truck, he re-tightened the battery cable on her convertible. Admittedly, it had been a stupid, asshole thing to do. He was not that desperate. His idiotic jealousy was getting in the way and could possibly ruin things with Colby if it hadn't already. And that jealousy drove him to where he stood presently.

He leaned over the intern's desk, flashing his bright white teeth as he gave her a big smile. She was a young college student who looked like she had put on the "freshman fifteen" and then some.

He wouldn't take no for an answer. "C'mon. I just need to go talk to my friend."

She gave him an uneasy look. "Sir—"

"Mace," he corrected her.

"Sir," she insisted, flushing. "I can't let you into the lab. Even if you are Martin's *friend*."

Mace never countered her idea he was Martin's "friend," but he wondered why she put the emphasis on "friend" every time she said it.

"C'mon...I need to surprise my buddy. It's his birthday!"

The girl's eyebrows shot up her forehead. "I didn't know it was Martin's birthday. And I didn't even get him a card." She stuck a thumbnail between her teeth and gnawed.

"I'm sure he won't mind. If you let me go in, I'll let him know you wished him a happy birthday."

"I'm sure you will..." She pursed her lips. "Okay, but if I get in trouble..." She nervously smoothed down her skirt as she left her desk and went over to the forbidden door—the locked door to the supposed secret inner sanctum.

"I promise you won't." Hopefully, he could keep his promise.

She held her keycard against the card reader mounted on the wall, and the lock clicked. Mace leaned over to give her chubby cheek a quick peck. He turned away before he could finish watching the flush crawl up her neck.

Heading down the narrow hallway, he read doorplates as he went. He hoped he didn't stumble across anyone since he didn't want any questions on why he skulked around the lab. When he came across an open doorway, he smiled. The nameplate read "Martin McConnell."

He slipped into the office before he could be detected and softly closed the door behind him. Just who Mace was looking for.

Martin looked up startled. "C-can I help you?"

He was nothing like Mace expected. The man's dirty-blond hair was tousled as if he ran his hand through it constantly. In fact, on one side, a part of it stuck straight out. And his hair had a purple tint to it.

What looked like a half-eaten peanut butter and jelly sandwich sat on his desk. Some of the grape jelly had squirted out of it, partially missing the paper towel it laid on. Mace didn't have to be an investigator to realize Martin was one messy dude. A large plop of jelly teetered on the formerly white lab coat that the man wore. He must wear more of his lunch than eat it.

Martin's glasses perched perilously on his face, the bridge riding down toward the end of his nose. Under the lab coat, he wore a robin's egg blue button down shirt with a deeper blue tie, but the tie showed old stains. Being a messy eater wasn't something new for this guy.

Pushing his glasses back up his nose, Martin rose to his feet. "Can I help you?" he asked again, sounding annoyed this time—as if he wasn't happy about the interruption.

"I'm Mace Walker."

After a slight hesitation, a knowing look replaced the puzzlement in the other man's face. He cleared his throat and extended his right hand. "Martin. Martin McConnell."

Mace stared at his extended hand. Peanut butter clung to his fingers. Martin followed his gaze.

"Oh. Sorry." He wiped his hand down the side of his lab coat, leaving a smear of the peanut spread. He extended it again, a bit cleaner this time.

Mace grasped his hand and gave it a firm shake. Martin's hand felt limper than a man's should have and reminded him of shaking hands with a woman.

"You're Colby's…uh…" A flush rose up Martin's neck.

"Yes, I am." Mace perched a hip on the cluttered desk. "Sit. Sit."

Martin sat. "What are you doing here? Visiting Colby?"

Mace gave him a crooked smile. "Actually, I came to see you."

"Oh." The assistant's eyebrows drew together. "Why?"

Mace spotted a corner of a photo frame buried under a pile of papers and dug it out. A kneeling man who was not Martin appeared in the photo, hugging a Golden Retriever. The dog was handsome. The man? Not so much. Not that he was any judge of how good looking men were. He barked out a loud cough—one deep enough to remind himself of his masculinity.

"Brother?" he asked a second later, turning the frame toward Martin, who shook his head.

"No. I'm sorry, why are you here?"

Mace tossed the frame on top of a mountain of files at the corner of the desk. "I just wanted to meet the man Colby...*hangs* out with all the time."

"Well, I don't know if I'd call it hanging out. We work together."

"And *hang* out together."

"Occasionally."

"Yes, you like to go to flea markets."

"Auctions," Martin clarified. "We both appreciate antiques and good deals."

"Marty—"

"Martin," he corrected, his glasses slipping precariously close to the end of his nose once again.

"*Martin*. Do I have anything to be concerned about?"

"I don't understand."

Apparently so. The guy's eyebrows knitted together so hard, they became a unibrow.

"Why did you send the roses?"

The unibrow rose to his hairline. "Roses? I don't know anything about roses."

"You didn't send a dozen roses to Colby?"

"No. Why would I?"

He almost said "to get a piece of ass" but instead he said, "She's a beautiful woman."

"Yes, she is. But…"

Mace waited. And waited. He watched the color in Martin's cheeks turn darker. The other man cleared his throat and fidgeted in his seat. If Mace kept silent long enough, the other man would spill the beans. Silence was a more effective investigation tool than drilling someone with questions.

Martin closed his eyes and blew out a breath. He grabbed the photo Mace had earlier and held it up. "If I was going to send anyone flowers, it would be him."

Shit. Now the quirk made sense. "Oh. Well…"

Mace stood up and paced in front of the desk. He, stupid ass that he was, had misjudged the relationship between Martin and Colby big time. *Fuck.* He was getting rusty. Sloppy. He had thought maybe Colby had a thing for nerds. Though Mace felt relieved he was wrong, since he certainly didn't fit in that category.

He stopped directly in front of the desk. Martin gave him a disapproving frown. "You thought Colby and I…That—"

"No. No." He dragged a hand through his hair. "Okay, maybe. I wasn't sure."

"We're just friends and co-workers."

Mace grimaced. Okay, now he had to do damage control. Martin was sure to run to Colby with this. And she wouldn't be happy.

Fuck! He would have to tell her first.

Damn. So, Martin wasn't the one. Now he didn't have a freaking clue who sent those flowers. That message. The subtle threat. He hoped it wasn't anyone in his past. No one should know he was back in town. Unless someone was looking for him. Or someone was looking for Colby.

Either way, he would keep an eye on her, make sure she stayed safe. He'd just have to suffer through it if it meant spending more time with her.

Mace smiled.

A HOT, steaming bag appeared beside Colby. It smelled wonderful. Lunch. Her stomach had growled all morning since she'd skipped breakfast.

"Thanks, Martin," she said, without even pulling her eyes away from the microscope. She slipped a pencil out of her lab coat pocket and jotted down some notes on a pad.

Martin didn't answer. When the hair on the back of her neck stood up, she sat back and glanced straight up at Mace. "What are you doing here?"

"What, no hello?"

What was he doing in her lab? "No!" She stood abruptly, making him catch her chair before it fell backward.

"I came to bring you lunch and deliver your car. I fixed it. Now I want my truck back."

"Fine." She dug into her lab coat pocket and held out his keys. "Here. Take them."

Mace reached for them and seized her hand instead. She tried to move away, but he held on tighter.

"Who let you in here? This area is off-limits to visitors."

"Martin let me in. We had a long talk."

"Why? What about?" She had a sinking feeling she knew.

"You. You didn't tell me about his sexual preference."

She cocked an eyebrow at him. "And he told you?"

Mace at least had the decency to look guilty when he said, "I don't think I left him a choice."

Colby finally tugged her hand away from his and sighed. "Oh, Mace. What's wrong with you? He's a good friend and co-worker. That's all."

"I realize that now." He pinned her with an accusing stare. "Why didn't you tell me he didn't like women? I mean...Well, you know what I mean."

"What does it matter?"

"I thought—"

"You shouldn't have thought! You were thinking with the wrong part of your body. Men!"

"Ouch, that's not fair."

"Fair? Is it fair you terrorize my co-worker?"

"No. I'm sorry." He took a step closer, making her take one back.

"Sorry!" She took another half-step back until her butt pressed against the counter. She had nowhere else to go, no way to escape.

"Yes, and believe it or not, I apologized to Martin. Hell, I even bought him lunch. He'll be gone for a while. I told him to take a nice, long lunch break." He moved closer, making her widen her stance to accommodate his larger body.

"You had no right." She jammed a hand against his chest when he leaned into her. *What the hell.*

He inclined close enough to place his lips on the shell of her ear and whisper, "I know, but I told him how hungry I was myself, and he understood."

Jesus. Heat licked at her cheeks. She'd never be able to look Martin in the eyes again.

His tongue barely brushed the edge of her ear, but just enough to make her want him. Why did he turn her on so easily? His thigh nestled between hers, and his erection pressed against her stomach. She shifted her hips, and her pelvis brushed against his good thigh. She bit her lip to muffle the cry she wanted, so wanted, to scream.

"You look really sexy in that lab coat. Have anything on underneath?"

"Yes," she hissed and twisted her head away. He would not be forgiven that easily. Nope.

He snagged her braid and turned her head back to him. His breath mingled with hers as he murmured, "Not for long," against her mouth.

Colby melted against the desk, and he took the opportunity to grind his thigh tight against her mound, just making enough movement to rub her clit.

"Ah...What are you going to do?"

Mace ran his tongue over her lips, dipping it for a quick touch of tongues before retreating. "Do you want me to tell you about it first or just do it?"

She had to get control of herself. She was a professional, for goodness' sake. "Mace. This is a lab!" she reminded him, as well as herself.

"I know. I'll bet it's one of your fantasies, isn't it?" He ran his hand under her lab coat and along her blouse until his thumb brushed one of her hard nipples. He circled, circled, circled, then pinched.

Colby's toes curled in her shoes. She might come still fully clothed. Not possible. "N-no. The door—"

"We're alone." He worked his other knee between her legs, making her spread them.

Lord, this man made her panties soaked. Her skirt shimmied its way up to the top of her thighs the farther he spread her legs apart. Pinning her to the counter with his hips, he thrust against her once, twice. Then his hands moved to the back of her thighs and he lifted her up so the edge of her ass was on the counter. He adjusted his hips once more so she could feel the length of his shaft against the soaked line of her panties.

"Mace...oh, oh shit...If we get caught..." Her heart thudded against her chest, and her breath came in quick pants. "This is not like the shooting range. I know these people; I work here."

She tried to slow her breathing, clear her head, but the hard line of his cock pressed in just the right spot.

"That's the excitement. Colby, I want you. I want you so badly, it hurts."

Her thighs quivered, and she felt a fresh rush of warmth between her legs. "Your leg..."

"Forget my leg. That's not what hurts."

"Oh, God." She groaned. "Mace..."

"I know, baby."

He unbuttoned her lab coat and then her blouse. He nuzzled her neck, right at the delicate spot behind her ear, before unclipping the clasp of her bra, releasing her breasts. Her puckered nipples ached as he lowered his head to stroke one with his tongue. A moment later, he gave the other nipple the same attention. The warm wetness combined with the rough texture of his tongue once again almost drove her over the edge. Digging her fingers into his hair, she kept him there while he sucked one then the other into his mouth—softly nipping, kisses quickly following the scrape of his teeth. She released a low, drawn-out moan.

This was torture. But torture never felt this good.

He impatiently pushed Colby farther back on the worktable, knocking her paperwork to the floor unnoticed. She wanted to protest, but when he slid a finger along the soaked edge of her panties, no words escaped. And when he drove one and then a second finger deep into her, she gasped. To hell with her paperwork.

"I'm," his fingers slid out and along her pussy lips, "just," they drove deep again, "going to," he curved his fingers deep within her, "take you," he stroked that spot, "right here," that sweet, sweet spot, "right now."

Colby gasped again and was about to come. Just when she felt the beginning of the contractions, his fingers disappeared. *Damn!* He ripped her panties down past her knees. She tried to kick them off, but they got caught on one ankle. She was in no position to fix the problem, and frankly, she didn't give a damn at that instant. She heard the zipper of his jeans then, *Oh...*the naked head of his cock slipped over her swollen clit, making her shudder. One tiny shift of her hips, and he would be inside her. He had to have read her thoughts, because he suddenly shifted, sliding his whole hard length against her heated flesh instead. His cock became slick with her arousal.

"Do you want it?" He plucked once more at her nipples.

"Yes."

"How much?"

"I—"

"How much?" he asked through gritted teeth.

Why was he delaying? "A—a lot."

"You are so fucking wet. Lift your hips."

He leaned back slightly when she did.

Colby tried to grab his hips with her legs to drag him closer. But he was fumbling with his jeans which were pulled down his hips. The denim framed his rigid cock, the dark curly hair, and his balls so nicely. But she didn't want to see how hard he was; she wanted to feel it. Inside her. "Now," she moaned.

"Not yet." He dug for his wallet.

"Now!"

"No." He grimaced and cursed when the wrapper refused to tear open.

"Mace…" She snagged the condom, ripped it open between her teeth and impatiently rolled it over his hot, steely length, stroking while she did it. When she reached the root of his cock, she cupped his balls and squeezed slightly.

"Christ, Colby!" he panted. He fisted his cock once, twice, and his whole body shuddered in response. He grabbed her wrist, breaking the contact of her nails lightly raking his balls. "Fuck!"

He held her hips tightly, tilted them a little higher, and with a grunt, he buried himself deep. As the breath whooshed out of both of them, Colby forgot how to breathe. He kept himself buried to the hilt and made small thrusting moves against her so his balls teased against her anus while his pelvis ground against her clit. The tiny thrusts drove her crazy. She needed to come. She couldn't take it much more.

With a grunt, he said, "Hold on."

"I can't—"

"Hold it." He dropped his forehead to her chest and gasped for air.

Her heart would thump right out of her chest if she didn't come soon. "Mace!"

He cursed, threw his head back while arching his back, and slammed his whole length into her again and again and again. Colby clawed at the counter, grabbing at nothing, and let out a low wail.

"Now!" He came with force, and her contractions drew him even deeper until they were both spent.

A moment later, he struggled to catch his breath. His chest heaved as he practically collapsed over her, the majority of his weight only held up by his forearms on the counter.

When his breath came more evenly, he kissed her nose, her eyelids, her lips, before licking the hollow of her collarbone. She was sure it tasted salty.

"Damn," she whispered when she caught her breath. "That was one hell of a lunch break."

Mace chuckled softly against her shoulder, still buried inside her. "Your food's getting cold."

She brushed the damp hair off his forehead. "I'm not hungry anymore."

CHAPTER 10

HE HAD PROMISED Colby he would meet her at the house. They planned to start painting the porch today, but Mace was running later than expected. The hardware store had been understaffed and busy. Even worse, his order of eight cans of paint didn't make them any happier, especially when he wanted them put in the shaker machine first. And that was *after* they had to mix the custom cream color Colby had fallen in love with.

At least she had enough paint at the house to get started before he got there. He could picture her already splattered with paint—in her fiery hair, on her clothes, covering the freckles on her cute nose.

As he steered his truck around the corner onto Colby's tree-lined street, he noticed the back end of an old car sticking out of her driveway. The overgrown brush lining the property's border concealed the rest. But there was enough of the vehicle exposed allowing Mace to recognize an early 90s Caprice. Primer gray.

He fought the urge to slam his foot on the gas, to hurry to the house, to get to Colby as soon as possible. Instead, he pulled over to the curb and collected himself. He jammed the gearshift in park before hopping out of his truck.

His instincts kicked in while he lurked along the edge of the property, staying close to the neighbor's side of the shrubbery. When he got to the back corner of the property, he climbed through the vegetation and carefully snuck through the back door of the house.

~

COLBY COULDN'T KEEP her mind off Mace no matter how hard she tried. She was happy. Really happy. At least for now. Every time she thought about having sex with him—the best sex of her life—at his house, at her house, at the lab, wherever, she practically melted into a puddle.

But he frustrated her too. One minute, he would do something to anger her, the next minute, he would turn around and make her heart—and pussy—ache. She was falling deep...

She tried to resist it. Resist him. But after only a couple weeks, she couldn't. She felt nothing like this before. Never. She was in love...with his lovemaking. Only that, she tried to convince herself. She swore to herself over a year ago she wouldn't fall into a similar trap again. She wouldn't break her own promise.

Though she would allow herself to enjoy Mace and all he offered for now. That was the limit. She'd enjoy his tenderness, his wildness, and his roughness. He didn't think he'd be around for more than a couple months. She would take those days. And those nights.

She painted the porch, making long, soothing strokes. Long, deep lines of color. Back and forth. Colby shut her eyes and took a deep, shaky breath. She pictured Mace's body above her, his cock hard and ready, nudging against her, opening her up—

"Hey, babe."

Colby froze, the paintbrush tumbling from her fingers. She helplessly watched it fall on the new porch floor and splatter. She couldn't move. Couldn't breathe. Nothing. But she closed her eyes once more and forced herself to take another deep breath. A slow, deep breath between trembling lips.

"What kind of welcome is that?"

The familiar male voice made her world spin. She clutched at the doorjamb to steady herself, her nails digging into the wood.

"Aren't you even going to turn around and give me a hug?"

His hand gripped her upper arm and, with force, spun her around. Colby opened her eyes and looked straight into Hell. *Craig.*

His dirty blond hair was still short and neatly trimmed. Blue eyes and lean muscle made up his six-foot frame; it was what had attracted her in the first place. But it wasn't just lean muscle, it was pure mean muscle. And like Mace, he could sweet-talk anyone wearing a skirt. But only when he wanted to.

"I've missed you something fierce."

Fierce wasn't the word. Evil was more like it. The reason she had purchased the gun and learned how to shoot it stood in front of her. He was the sole reason she left her hometown—where she had been born and lived her whole life—to move here. Her little new-found heaven was fast becoming her living hell. Once again.

"Cat got your tongue?" he purred. He reached out, brushing a knuckle down her cheek.

She bit back a whimper. If she showed even a sliver of fear, he would only be more brutal.

He liked fear. He fed off her terror. She shook her head, dislodging his hand.

This was not happening. She had been painting too long, and the fumes had affected her. She only imagined this. Right? Right? *Right!*

Wrong.

Craig Jones lowered his head, bringing him only a hairsbreadth away, and inhaled deeply. "Your hair smells so good, babe. Damn, have I missed you."

"C-Craig. What are you doing here? How did you find me?"

He laughed. To Colby's ears it sounded cruel, biting. "It wasn't hard. There aren't too many places where a biochemist can find a job."

"Why?" She pinned herself against the doorjamb, trying to get as far away from him as possible. He shifted closer, tilting his head. He planted one hand on the doorjamb, fingers close enough to grab her French braid in a split second.

"Why? What a silly question. I just told you. I miss you." He gave her a cold smile.

"What happened to Rhonda?"

"Rhonda." He shook his head and smirked. "I don't care about her. I don't want her anymore. I want *you* back."

Her heart squeezed as if she might go into cardiac arrest. Hell, she *wanted* to have a heart attack. *Anything.* Anything to get away from this man.

I want you back.

I want you back.

I want you back.

"No," Colby whispered and slid down the jamb to the floor.

Craig grabbed her wrists and dragged her back up, his face a cruel mask just inches away. He continued to pull her arms until they stretched out above her, her wrists pinned to the door molding. He held them so tightly, her fingers quickly became numb.

"No? Why not, babe? We were good together. You loved me! I loved you. I still do."

Something inside her snapped. She shouldn't provoke him, but she couldn't stop herself. She couldn't help but poke at the beehive.

"Craig, you *loved* me? Is that why you hit me? Kicked me? Broke my ribs and my arm? You almost loved me to death!"

"I only hit you, babe, because you frustrated me with all your distrust and accusations!"

She laughed, which even sounded insane to her own ears. "Oh God, Craig. You had other women behind my back. Why should I have trusted you? All my accusations were true."

"But, babe, they meant nothing. I only loved you." He said it so slowly, Colby fought to keep the contents in her stomach down. This man was psychotic. Fate had played an evil trick on her when it brought him into her life.

Craig released her wrists so suddenly, she fell back against the house siding. Her head cracked against the corner of the jamb. She ignored the pain, needing to show strength, not weakness. Otherwise, she was finished. He would never forgive her for leaving him, for sneaking away during the night from the hospital.

He strode away from her before spinning around to pin her with his stare. "You don't love me anymore?"

She clenched her fingers into fists and wanted to spit in his face. "No. I haven't loved you since the first time you blackened my eye."

"Colby, babe, I apologized for all that. I told you I'd never do it again. I promised."

Hysterical laughter bubbled up. *I promised.* How many times had she heard those empty promises? She heard them until her ears rang from his slaps.

She glanced wildly toward the driveway at her parked car. Inside was the gun. And she wanted to blow this son of a bitch away.

But, she would never make it to the car. Never. She took a deep breath to fortify herself. "This is my property, Craig. I don't want you on it."

He gave her a lopsided smile. "Babe, please, you don't mean it."

"Craig, I'm warning you. Get the hell off my property before—"

"Before what? What are you going to do? Who's going to stop me?"

"Me."

That single word—those two little letters—brought a sense of salvation to Colby.

Holy shit. Mace's deep timbre never sounded so good. She could feel his presence behind her in the open doorway. His strength, his presence, was all she needed. She never needed him as much as she needed him that moment.

She needed him, and he was there. *He was there.*

"And who the hell are you?" Craig shouted. His chest puffed out, and he slammed his hands on his hips, taking a step closer to her.

"Your worst nightmare. Believe me, asshole, I've dealt with more low-life, scum- sucking pigs than you. And let me tell you, I've squashed them like bugs. If you don't believe me, just try me. I'll enjoy breaking every goddamn bone in your fucking body."

Mace stepped around Colby and right into Craig's face. He blocked her with his body. His voice lowered to a deep grumble. "If you ever, *ever* come or ever even think about coming on this property or bothering Colby again...*I swear*...you will never walk again. Never. And that's no idle threat."

Colby didn't doubt his words. Apparently, neither did Craig.

For the first time, she saw her ex shrink in fear. She had done it so many times herself. Now, the tables had turned.

"Now, you better get the hell out of here. If I ever see your face again, mine will be the last you ever see." Mace's words cut like cold steel, making it clear he wasn't a man to be messed with.

Colby shuddered as she heard the tremendous strength in those words. Feeding off of it, she stood straighter and stared Craig directly in the eyes. "You'd better go, Craig, if you know what's good for you. Let me make something real clear before you go. I'm not interested. Stay out of my life."

"Yeah, I see. You've got yourself a new man," Craig sneered while he backed down the porch steps. If he'd been a dog, his tail would have been tucked between his legs.

They stood silently until he was out of sight.

The silence felt tense, though, and violent energy still permeated from Mace's body. She waited.

"Who the fuck was that?"

Colby recoiled. She couldn't deal with his anger. Not now. She needed him to hold her while she sobbed in relief until she couldn't cry anymore.

"Colby! Look at me! Why didn't you tell me about him? Why didn't you warn me?"

"I...I didn't think he'd find me. Or even want to find me."

Mace stood stiffly, clenching and unclenching his fists. "Unbelievable. What if I hadn't been here? What then, Colby?"

She pressed the back of her hand against her trembling lips. "I don't know. I was too far away from my gun."

He shot her an incredulous look. "Your gun? That's why you have one? *Jesus Christ!* I mean…I knew someone hurt you. I knew it." He fumed and paced the porch. "I just didn't realize it was physically. Fucking bastard," he ground out. "What were you going to do, Colby? Shoot him?"

"I don't know."

"Yes, you do. You would have killed him if you had the chance."

He was right. She would have. "Yes."

Mace groaned and pulled her to him, wrapping his arms around her and rocking her back and forth. Her body shuddered, stiffened, then finally melted as a sob escaped her.

"I hate him."

"I know," he whispered into her hair. He smoothed his hands up and down her back, hugging her tighter. "He's gone now."

"He might come back." She shivered and sniffled. His T-shirt became damp with her tears. She was acting foolish, but she couldn't help it.

"He won't. I promise." Mace placed his lips on her forehead. Colby knew the promise was good; Craig would never come back. She was sure being a federal agent he could "make some calls." But, honestly, she didn't care what happened to the bastard.

As she attempted to wipe her tears away with the back of her hand, he stopped her and kissed them away with his lips.

"How much did you hear?" she asked, her voice still shaky.

"Enough." He sat down on the top porch step and enveloped her in his arms. "You should have told me."

"I couldn't."

"Why?"

"I…" Fresh tears rolled down her cheeks. There was no point in not being truthful with him. "I felt ashamed."

"You told no one?"

Colby shook her head.

Mace's jaw clenched, she heard him suck in a breath, then felt the tension suddenly leave his body as quickly as it had come. "Colby, let's go home."

I am home, she thought when he held her even tighter.

MACE LEANED back against the living room couch, his bare feet propped up on the coffee table, the evening news blaring from the TV in the background. Colby sat next to him quietly while he finished scanning the legal document in his hands.

He gave a bitter laugh and threw the PFA onto the table in front of him. "What a fucking joke. You know those protection orders are useless, don't you? What do they expect you to do? Throw it at him? Give him a paper cut?"

"It's better than nothing, I guess." She'd been told the Protection From Abuse order would, well, protect her. She'd been grossly misled.

"Yeah, shit, it really helped you out today, didn't it?" He made a fist in his lap. "Even if you could've dialed 911, he could have seriously hurt you or even kidnapped you before any local donut-lover would have arrived on scene. Those pieces of paper can't stop a bullet."

"It was stupid of me not to have my cell phone nearby."

"I'm sorry. I don't mean to make this worse. Don't blame yourself. You're doing what you should be: moving on and living your life."

He picked up his beer bottle from the side table, took one long swig, then one more, before placing it back on the "FBI: Female Body Inspector" coaster. He said the coasters were a gag gift from his sister when he had graduated from the Academy.

"Where's the rest of it?"

Without even asking, she knew what he wanted. She leaned over and picked up the folder she'd thrown on the floor next to the couch.

She offered it to him without a word. He took it and laid it in his lap, not even opening it.

Instead, he studied her face while he asked, "Are these copies or originals?"

"A little of each."

"Do you really want me to see them?"

Without hesitation, she answered him truthfully. "No."

"But you'll let me look at them," he said, his expression shuttered.

"Yes."

She grabbed her wine glass from the table by his feet and finished off the two remaining swallows. It was false hope; she didn't think the alcohol would help her get through this. This amounted to picking at a healing wound. She didn't want to relive it.

He finally tore his gaze away from her face and opened the folder. When he picked up the first photo, Colby looked away. She didn't need to look at the pictures to remember. All she had to do was close her eyes, and she couldn't forget.

She turned her attention to the TV, trying to concentrate on a news piece about a town councilman getting into hot water.

"*Jesus Christ.*" What started out as a shocked whisper ended up not a minute later as an explosive, "*That motherfucker!*"

He whipped the folder across the room, the dozens of photos spilling like confetti over the carpet. One landed at her feet, and her own face, hardly recognizable due to the swelling and discoloration, stared back at her. Colby closed her eyes, willing back the tears.

"I'm sorry. I'm sorry." He pushed himself up and went around the room collecting the photos, jamming them back into the folder. Picking the PFA off the coffee table, he shoved it into the folder as well before throwing the whole thing onto the seat of the nearby recliner.

He settled back beside her on the couch and took another long pull at his beer. "I'm sorry, Colby."

She wanted to ask him for what, but she wasn't sure she really wanted to know. He was probably sorry she'd made herself a victim.

He was probably sorry she didn't leave Craig sooner. He was probably sorry she'd been too weak to protect herself from harm. He might be sorry she'd been so desperate to love somebody, she'd picked the wrong person. Maybe he was just sorry he lost his temper and threw her folder, her painful reminder, across the room.

"I'm sorry you were hurt like that. I wish I found you a lot sooner." The last was said softly, so softly, it tugged strongly at her. She wished she'd met him a lot sooner as well.

"Your battle scars are much worse," she reminded him.

He hesitated for a few long heartbeats, what looked like sadness softening his eyes. "I got mine from someone who hated me enough to want me dead. Yours came from someone who supposedly loved you."

"Maybe we're all misled."

"About what?"

"About love. Maybe we're so desperate for someone's affections, we see a connection where there isn't any."

"Maybe. But I think love's possible. I think it's out there for the right people." Running a hand down her jawline, he tucked some escapees from her braid behind her ear. "My parents loved each other deeply. I saw it every day in the way they acted and talked to each other. Sometimes, it was as small as just a look between the two. But it was enough even a teenage boy would notice. After my father died, my mother became so heartbroken, she died not two months later."

"She died of a broken heart?"

"Something like that." He cupped her face and leaned in to kiss her.

"I didn't think it was possible."

"I'm starting to think it is." He kissed her lightly, nudging her lips open, his tongue exploring.

She didn't want to read into his comment. She didn't want things to become complicated. Hell, she didn't want to admit they had already. She kissed him back, her tongue wrestling with his before she broke away, kissing down his chin. His shadow of a beard felt rough against her lips.

Colby's lips moved along his jaw, then her tongue ran a line down his neck, leaving a warm, moist trail.

This was exactly what he needed after this afternoon's incident—to get his mind off what might have happened to Colby. If he hadn't been in the picture…

Shit.

She nipped at where his shoulder met his neck, and he leaned his head against the back of the couch, enjoying every second, giving her every opportunity to do what she wanted with him. He was all hers.

She kissed, nipped, and licked here and there over his neck. She pushed his T-shirt up, exposing his chest to continue her teasing pattern over and around his nipples. He leaned forward, grabbed the back of his shirt, and ripped it over his head. He tossed it onto the recliner, covering that fucking folder. Once again, it reminded him of what might have, could have happened.

But it hadn't, and here they were: about to have a little bit of fun with each other. Or a whole hell of a lot of fun, if it was up to him.

He lost his train of thought when she raked her nails lightly over his nipples.

"Fuck." He grabbed the end of her braid as she diligently rubbed and kissed all over his stomach and chest. Pulling the small elastic band off the end, he combed his fingers through the plait, untangling her hair from its confines. He worked his way up while she worked her way down, following the line of his dark hair to the top of his jeans. The button was already unfastened since he never finished securing his jeans after his shower earlier.

He caught her studying him while she slowly unzipped his jeans. He probably looked as dumbfounded as he felt. He doubted any blood remained in his brain, it seemed it all headed south into his shaft.

Colby sat back suddenly and gave him a stern look. "Take off your pants." It wasn't a request. Hell no, it wasn't. "Now."

Damn, if he could get any harder than he already was...Impossible.

He pushed to his feet and caught himself as he lost his balance. His thigh protested loudly. But he didn't give a shit. Not tonight.

Tomorrow, he would pay for it. But tonight, he'd get his money's worth, even if he had to do PT twice a day for the next week.

He pushed his jeans down to his knees before sitting back on the couch to yank them the rest of the way off, tossing them somewhere into the room. He had gone commando, skipping the boxer briefs tonight hoping to get lucky. So he sat there naked, his cock as erect as a flagpole. All he needed was the redheaded vixen in front of him to raise the flag.

His flag raiser didn't say a word. Her eyes had softened momentarily when he'd stumbled but had quickly gone back to stern. It reminded him of the first night he came home. He pictured her again like the school teacher: stern, prim, and proper on the outside, wild as hell on the inside.

She pushed herself off the couch and moved to stand in between his open knees, not touching, though. She leveled her gaze at him— no smile, eyes serious. Her expression alone kept him from fisting his own aching cock.

A moment later, she shook her head. Her hair flew wildly around her shoulders and down her back. She undid her jeans and slipped out of them, but he couldn't tell if she wore any panties since her long, collared shirt hung halfway down her thighs. But, it was still sexy as hell.

Damn, he wanted to fuck the shit out of her. But he didn't reach out. Instead, he waited to see what her game was. The anticipation would kill him, but he loved it.

She licked her lips, he thought more out of nervousness than teasing. But when one hand started unbuttoning her shirt while the other went to her mouth, he questioned his own theory. She slid one finger between her lips, sucked on it, then slowly drew it back out.

He didn't know where to look: the finger she teased with her tongue or the ones working the buttons out of their confinement. Her shirt gaped enough now he could get a glimpse of a dark green bra, almost the same color as her eyes.

He didn't have to decide what to look at when she slid her wet finger down her gaping shirt and into her panties. He might not see it, but he sure could imagine it.

That jolted him into wrapping a fist around his shaft, which was leaking already, the precum beading on the crown.

Colby paused and gave a sharp "No."

Mace jerked at her tone, surprised it came from her, and automatically released his cock.

Damn.

But he would not complain. If she wanted all the control tonight, well, he wouldn't fight it.

She continued unbuttoning her shirt one-handed, and when the last one was released, her open shirt revealed enough he could see her other hand was definitely, *definitely*, down her panties. Which happen to be the same color and fabric as her bra, but he didn't care about that. He only cared about what was happening beneath the green fabric. He could see her fingers moving, knuckles shifting, her wrist sliding under the cotton. She ran her free hand over her bra, pushing the shirt to the side more, giving him a better view. She threw her head back and gasped.

Then her legs buckled. Before he could reach out to keep her from falling, she dropped to her knees and grasped his ankles, making him jump at the unexpected contact.

She traced her fingers up both of his calves, past his bent knees and over his thighs, being careful of his injury. She moved herself closer, pressing in between his legs, while she slid her hands around his hips, over his clenched stomach, and lower, once again. Two fingers circled the root of his cock, and she squeezed.

Mace pressed his lips together to keep from babbling like an idiot while his stomach clenched even harder, and his fingers dug into the couch cushion. One reason was he didn't want to come. The other was to keep from dragging her up and over his lap to impale her deep.

The two fingers circling his cock became her whole hand as she leaned over his lower body.

Christ, nothing excited him more than seeing her fire-red hair in his lap. It brushed against his thighs, swept against his groin, and tickled his lower stomach. He might come if she kept brushing her hair against his cock. So silky—

He sucked in a breath, and his hips rose off the couch when her hot little mouth enclosed over the head of his cock. Her tongue whisked away all of his precum, like a kitten lapping up cream. She took him all the way in, almost to the root. Her lips bumped against her own fist before sliding back up to the top, her tongue teasing the small slit for a moment before her hot, hot, *hot* mouth took almost his whole length again.

Oh. Fuck. Me.

When she shot him a look, he realized he might have said that out loud. Not even a moment later, she picked up a rhythm with her tongue and her lips, stroking his length while her fist squeezed his root.

He leaned his head back and couldn't watch; if he did, he might lose it. He didn't have to see what she was doing. Hell no. The vision was burned in his brain. He would remember this for a long time.

When her other hand gently cupped his balls and squeezed, his eyes flew open and he heard someone cry out. That someone was him.

His brain became so addled, she could tell him to jump and he wouldn't even ask her how high. He would do anything, anything, she told him to. Especially when she licked the head like a Tootsie Pop, trying to see how many licks it took to get to the center. He was either very tasty, or she was very hungry…

Her steady rhythm down his length began again, and he couldn't resist: he sank his fingers into her hair and began to thrust. His hips rose to meet her at every stroke. His fingers tightened in her hair, and he tensed, ready to blow his load. He needed release. His balls became so freaking tight, and it didn't help she continued to play with them, squeeze them, roll them between her slender fingers.

She pulled her head away and said, "No, I want you to come inside me."

She looked beautiful with her flushed cheeks and her glistening lips swollen. He would have been happy coming right where he was. But she decided to be the boss.

And so she shall be.

She climbed to her feet and stepped back from between his legs, just out of reach. Her shirt slid to the floor, and she stood, looking oh-so-edible in her matching green bra and panties. Panties that now appeared a little darker at the apex of her legs. And that made him smile.

"I need help."

Mace lifted one eyebrow in question. He wanted it to look roguish, but the truth was, he couldn't get any words past the lump in his throat.

"I want you to take these off," she said, turning away from him. She stepped back closer to him before lifting her hair up and out of the way.

He ran his fingers over the smooth, fair skin of her back, along the edge of her shoulder straps before reaching for the clasp. He popped it open and let her bra fall away to the front.

He ran his palms down her sides until he reached the top of her panties, then he slid his fingers under the edge of the elastic and around to the front, almost hugging her waist. With his hands back at her hips, he pushed them down. Slowly. His touch lingered here, there—over her hips, down her thighs, past her knees, until the green scrap of fabric dropped to her ankles. She lifted one foot out before kicking the panties away with the other.

Still with her back to him, she crossed her arms over her breasts, her hair covering her back like a cape of fire. She couldn't be shy now. She lost her inhibitions during sex, she didn't get more. So she couldn't be hiding herself from him.

And, *oh shit*, she wasn't.

When she turned to face him, she kneaded her own breasts, plucking both nipples, her lower lip caught between her teeth. She worked one hand down her stomach, once again to the fiery patch below, and parted her pussy lips...

"Don't—" he blurted out, making her pause. "Oh, fuck, don't," he groaned and then cursed himself.

"You don't like?"

"Oh, no, I like. I like a lot. But I will end up losing it all over myself."

"Scoot back."

He did. He pressed himself to the back of the couch and offered his hands to her. She accepted and used his arms for balance while she climbed over him, placing a knee on each side of his hips. He caught a whiff of her scent, hot and musky and so freaking female. He wanted to bury his face between her legs and taste her. But that wasn't how it would go tonight. Tonight, she was in charge.

She lingered above him, putting her weight on her shins. She was so far above him. Too far. She needed to be closer. Much closer.

"Condom?" he squeaked. He held onto her upper arms, making sure she didn't lower herself yet. Not until some important business was taken care of first.

"I have it covered."

"Okay, uh..."

Colby leaned forward and placed her lips by his ear, whispering, "I've been on birth control, but I wasn't sure before... Now, I am. I want just you, only you, inside me, nothing in between us."

Mace groaned in anticipation; it sounded like a good plan to him. What a great fucking plan. The best he'd ever heard. His cock jerked, and it brushed against her damp curls, which made him thrust his hips up in response.

Colby laughed huskily. "Down, boy."

Bracing a hand against his chest for balance, she grabbed his shaft with the other, rubbing it against her slit, making it even slicker, if possible. She lined it up in perfect position, and he was ready, so ready to send it home.

She made small circles with her hips, lowering herself. She'd go down one inch, come back up until only the tip entered her, go down two inches, and come back up. Then down three inches before coming back up, all the while keeping her inner muscles tight and circling her hips.

He was going to pass out. Any second now, he would just drop over dead. With the biggest fucking grin on his face, too.

When she finally sank down on him, swallowing him whole, he lost his train of thought. He wrapped his arms around her back and held her there. She ground circles against his lap, and he pressed his face between her breasts, air hissing from his lungs. He struggled to catch his breath when she rocked against him, letting out little mews and gasps. Her sounds vibrated through her chest against his cheek as he nuzzled her chest, moving until he caught a nipple in his mouth, drawing down on the tight, hard nub. The faster she rocked, the harder he sucked.

Suddenly, her movements became frantic, and within seconds, she stiffened, clenching her inner muscles around him and letting out a long wail. He thrust up and felt the heat rolling through him. He released himself deep within her, his cock jerking along with her orgasm.

He thanked his lucky stars that she came so quickly. Because he wouldn't have held out much longer.

When Colby collapsed against his chest, she wrapped her arms around his neck, sighing. "Wow," she whispered into his hair.

He chuckled. "Ditto." Nuzzling her neck, he kissed along her damp skin.

She said, "I need to get off your leg." Though she made no effort to do so.

"No. You're fine. I don't want you to move." His leg only spasmed slightly. It would settle down soon.

The phone rang, making Colby jerk against him. She eyed the phone worriedly. "How about now?"

"Still fine." He stretched over and plucked the cordless phone from the side table. "Hello?" Silence greeted him. He tried one more time. "Hello?" A soft laughter answered him before he heard a click and the dial tone. Mace's stomach dropped.

He pushed the "End" button on the phone and slammed it on the tabletop. "Well, we now know who *wasn't* making those calls."

He needed to call the phone company and cancel the service. Then go out back with all the phones in the house and take a sledgehammer to them.

Colby's arms tightened around him, and she buried her face against his neck. He traced his fingers up and down the crease of her spine.

At first, he'd hoped some stupid kid pranked the house. After Craig had showed up, he'd hoped it had just been that bastard. But he was getting a very bad feeling about this. He was at the point now where he might have the Bureau trace the calls.

He cupped Colby's ass cheeks. He wanted to get to the bottom of this soon.

CHAPTER 11

COLBY WALKED through the aisles of what, at first glance, looked like junk. It wasn't, though. Antiques and other household items lay in long rows on the grass. Every so often, something—a unique piece of furniture or knickknack—would catch her eye, and she would hesitate, investigate, and inspect.

If she liked it, it would go on her list along with what she thought it was worth, or at least, what her limit would be while bidding. With limited funds to furnish the house, she had to keep her spending under control. Renovations were her priority. Having a non-leaking roof over her head was more important than an antique settee.

As it was, auctions had a tendency to get her caught up in the moment, and before she knew it, she had spent way too much on an item. Auctions were fun, but addicting.

She couldn't believe Mace wanted to come with her and Martin today. Recently, he'd been sticking close to her. Any time she needed to run an errand, he would either insist on doing it for her or at least want to go along.

She didn't know if he was trying to be helpful or just being overly possessive. Either way, he tagged along today. But not long after arriving, Martin and Mace wandered away talking about what pieces of furniture would go nicely with the wainscoting and wood molding in her house.

Normally, she preferred the auctions held during the week and during the day, because those usually had less competition for an item she wanted. However, this auction was loaded with people, because it was a beautiful Saturday morning.

The property was only about a mile away from hers, and the auction was held by the estate of the late owner. The house itself was being auctioned off, but it was in very bad shape, even worse than hers had been when she bought it. Whoever bought it today would most likely have to tear it down and start over. But though the house appeared in disarray, the old wood furniture had been well kept. Classic, stunning pieces littered the yard.

As she strolled down another aisle, she found a particular piece she'd seen listed in the auction catalog: a beautiful Victorian dresser made from a burl of walnut.

She pulled open a drawer to inspect the dovetailing. The mirror was large, and the wood around the glass was hand carved. The white molded and variegated marble top made a stunning contrast with the rich walnut color of the wood. It was in excellent condition for a piece of furniture which had survived since the 1860s.

Colby stepped back to stare at it. She really wanted it but knew it would bring a hefty price. She sighed in disappointment. Some collector would snap it up at a price way out of her range.

"Beautiful, isn't it?"

She jumped at the deep male voice which came from right over her shoulder and spun to face the stranger. "Yes. I'd love it, but I don't think I'll be able to afford it."

"How do you know you can't afford it? This is an auction. Deals can always be found at an auction."

The tall but stocky man had dark brown eyes, and his hair was just as dark. His complexion was darker than Mace's, more olive-toned, and unmistakably ethnic even though he didn't have an accent. Something about him made her uncomfortable. Maybe because he stood too close and invaded her personal space.

Colby sidestepped to put a little more room between them. She shrugged. "I've seen what similar pieces have gone for. I'm not holding out hope to win this."

"But you'll bid?"

She thought a moment. "Yes, until it passes my budget."

"Which is?"

She didn't feel comfortable talking money with a complete stranger, so she skirted the question. "What pieces are you interested in?"

He gave a slight shrug, then buried his hands into the pockets of his slacks. But not before she noticed the expensive watch on his wrist. Rolex. Could be a knock-off.

"I'm just here to observe."

Observe? That was a bit odd. Most people at auctions came because they either wanted a good deal or a particular item, not just to observe. "Are you related to the estate?"

"No. I was just driving by when I saw the cars and the auction sign. I figured I'd check it out."

Yes, there were a lot of cars parked haphazardly—on the street, on the lawn, blocking the neighbors' driveways. Just a typical auction day. But this road wasn't a thoroughfare, a cut-through, or even typically used for commuting. "So, you're from the area?"

Those dark eyes, suddenly cold, pinned her for a moment, and Colby fought the urge to shiver. Why would a simple question like that bother him?

"No. I'm just visiting...friends." He tilted his head and slowly ran his gaze over her as if she were one of the precious antiques up for bid.

Unable to fight it this time, a shiver shot up her spine. And it wasn't from him showing an interest in her. A "something was off" feeling overcame her. Though, she couldn't put her finger on it. She feigned interest in the dresser's mirror, running her fingers around the serpentine carving.

"Exquisite woodwork, yes?" he asked.

Without answering, Colby looked up into the mirror. The man stood directly over her right shoulder, but over her left, she spotted Martin and Mace. They stood only two aisles away, deep in conversation. In fact, it looked like they were debating over a claw foot tub.

Would it be really obvious if she turned and started frantically waving them over?

But, luckily, she didn't have to. Mace glanced up suddenly, as if he'd felt her gaze and her silent plea. He spotted the man near her, straightened, and began walking quickly toward her, no indication of a limp in his determined stride.

If she wasn't concerned before about this stranger, she was now. Mace's expression looked a bit panicked, and his body language showed a bit of urgency. He was struggling to hide both, but failing miserably.

For him to be an undercover federal agent and have his emotions shown so clearly…

Which just proved she needed to move, and she needed to move now. Standing there like a dope wasn't going to do her any good if this man wanted to hurt her. But…what the hell? Why would this guy want to hurt her?

She turned to face the man. He'd disappeared. Just like that, poof. She glanced around but couldn't find him, even in the nearby aisles.

Mace rushed up to her and grabbed her upper arm more firmly than necessary.

"Ow. What's going on?"

His gaze searched the area, and he pulled her tightly against him. Martin made his way toward them, dodging other auction attendees who gathered near the podium anticipating the start of the auction.

"Who was that?" Mace asked her, finally giving her all of his attention.

"I have no idea. Just some auction attendee, I guess." At least that was what she had thought. Now, she wasn't so sure.

"Did he tell you his name?"

"No. Should he have?" Mace didn't answer. He went back to eyeballing the crowd. "Mace, what the hell is going on?"

He visibly relaxed and lightly brushed his lips over her forehead as if placating her.

Like something so simple would do it.

"Nothing. A bit of jealousy."

He lied. He might be good at it, but it was obvious to her. He was not the type of man who would ever admit being jealous. Never.

"Martin and I had an interesting conversation," he blurted, obviously trying to change the subject.

"Oh?"

"Yeah." He grabbed her elbow and steered her away from the crowd. He moved her toward a stretch of trees and some privacy. Once there, he pinned her back against a tree, out of the view from the rest of the crowd. "He told me something that disturbed me," Mace said, his face just fractions of an inch away from hers.

She was still trying to wrap her brain around the sudden change in subject. Distracting her would not work. "Okay, are you going to keep me in suspense? Or are you going to tell me?"

"He knew all about Craig."

Crap. Maybe distracting her *would* work. "Well, he's my friend, my co-worker. I confided in him."

"But you couldn't tell me about him. You couldn't warn me."

"I told you why." Craig wasn't a topic she liked to talk about since he was an embarrassing part of her past—one she wanted to forget, especially now Mace ran him off.

"You didn't feel comfortable enough with me to tell me." Not a question, but a statement.

Okay, this bothered him more than she ever would have thought. "Jesus, Mace. Are you really so bent out of shape about it?"

He didn't say anything for a long moment, just studied her face.

Then he lowered his head until their lips met. At first, it was a soft kiss, but it became more urgent. He buried his fingers into her braid, twisting his mouth over hers, dipping his tongue between her lips. His knee pushed between her thighs until it pressed against her mound. In an instant, he was grinding his thigh against her clit, making her moan into his mouth.

He pulled back a fraction, his breath mingling with hers. "Damn it, Colby, I want you to trust me."

She didn't answer. She wanted to trust him, too.

He blew out a breath and tucked a strand of stray hair behind her ear before giving her a reassuring smile. "Come on. We have to see if we can get some stuff to fill up that big, empty house of yours." With that, he pushed away from her and headed back toward the crowd.

He was trying to cover up his fear about something. It was more than her just having a random conversation with a stranger. And not knowing what bothered him worried her.

CHAPTER 12

MACE REACHED out to beat on the annoying object. The vibrating cell phone once again danced over the smooth surface of the nightstand. Reluctantly, he picked it up and put it to his ear. "What?"

Dead silence greeted him until he realized he held the phone upside down. He righted it and repeated his gruff greeting.

"Keep an eye out, Walker. We've been getting reports—reliable ones—Spinozi and his men are looking for you."

If that wasn't a wake-up call, Mace didn't know what was. He sat up slightly, leaning back against the headboard. "Wait, wait." He glanced over at the pillow next to him to make sure Colby was still asleep. Cupping his hand around his mouth and the cell, he whispered, "Okay, what the hell is going on?"

"There's a price on your head."

Well, wonder of all wonders. "A hit? What's the prize?"

"You'll never guess."

"So just tell me."

"Two and a half."

"Thousand?"

The man on the other end chuckled.

"Hundred thousand?" Mace still didn't get a response. He shook his head in disbelief. "No."

"Yes. I'm almost tempted to kill you myself."

Mace dragged a hand through his disheveled hair. "Two and a half million? Holy shit, Spinozi must be really pissed."

"Hmm. I'd say that's an understatement. I hope you're healing rapidly because I hate to tell you, you're on your own, buddy. I would send a couple men out to cover you, but I have no one to spare. And anyway, you're twice as good as my second best man. I figured you'd be able to handle this little snag on your own."

"Little snag?" A little snag was not being shot in cold blood by a Mafia kingpin's goon.

"For your sake and hers, get rid of the girl and think about getting yourself to a safe house. The contract is fresh, so if they don't know about her already, she'll be okay. But don't wait. It's only a matter of time."

Mace softly cursed when the phone went dark. He tucked it under his pillow and turned to watch Colby sleep. Her breathing remained deep and steady, so he had no reason to think she heard any of it.

Damn. How was he going to get her out of his life? These last few weeks had been the best weeks he'd ever had. Colby was great...sexy and smart...Hell, the sex was unbelievable. Biochemist by day, sex kitten by night. She was open to his suggestions, willing to try something new every night. Every morning, too.

However, he paid the price of their daily romper room. During the day when she was at work, his physical therapist worked out the intense leg cramps he had due to the increased activity. Robin told him he ought to stop torturing himself; he told her to forget it. The cramps were worth it, even if Colby didn't know what a strain it put on him.

Shit. What was he going to do? Break it off with her? He couldn't do it. He had to think. How could he keep her safe but still in his life?

Fuck. He couldn't.

146

That little run-in with the stranger at the auction was proof enough he couldn't protect her 24/7. The guy might have been some random stranger, but...

He didn't want to think about the "but."

Damn, he would have to separate himself from her, and in a way she wouldn't figure out the real reason either. He couldn't tell her he had a contract on his head. The last thing he wanted was for her to panic. If someone just pranking the house stressed her out the way it had...

Well, maybe it was to be expected. She originally thought it had been Craig doing it. He couldn't blame her for being scared of the bastard after what he'd seen in those photos.

But it would be better for her not to be frightened. For herself. For him. She could live her life safely and securely now she finally had Craig Jones out of her life. But with Spinozi putting contracts out on his head, her little safe world might come crashing down. And she deserved better. So much better.

If Spinozi had any idea how he felt about Colby, the fat bastard wouldn't hesitate knocking her off. Or worse.

Okay, think, think, think. How could he suddenly distance himself without getting an interrogation from her?

What would be plausible after everything that happened between the two of them? They had gotten into a routine: her working during the week while he went to PT, dinner together at night, down and dirty dessert later in the evening, weekends at her house fixing it up.

Mace groaned. He would have to be a cold-hearted bastard. He would have to get into character and become something, someone she hated.

He would have to become Craig.

Fuck! Why did he have to do this? If there were any other way...

Colby's arm reached over him as she stretched. The sheet slipped away, exposing a bare breast. He closed his eyes against the temptation. Maybe he could wait to...No, he needed to do it now. She didn't deserve to be tangled in his mess.

Rolling onto her side, she gave him a wide smile. "Good morning."

He did not want to do this. He really didn't. He took a deep breath, looking down into her glowing face. Squeezing his eyes shut for a moment, he reluctantly slipped into character.

"Is it?" He kept his voice clipped and cold.

Confusion crossed her face, her eyebrows knitting together. "Is something wrong?"

"What could be wrong? Everything's just perfect. Everything is going the way you'd like." He got out of bed, turning to point a finger at her. "Why don't you just move your things in here? Why do you even need your own room? Hell, why are you even bothering to fix up that deathtrap of a house?"

She tugged the sheet up over her chest, her face pale. "Mace, what's wrong? Does your leg hurt? Did I do something?"

"I've got to shower. Aren't you going to be late for work?"

She glanced wide-eyed at the clock. "No."

"Then why aren't you downstairs making me breakfast?"

Mace stormed out of the bedroom, leaving Colby alone in his bed, her jaw hanging.

He slammed the bathroom door behind him and paced. He needed time to get a plan together, to make this believable. If he fucked this up, it could be her death sentence. Or his.

After he'd got out of the shower and dressed, he stomped down the stairs and into the kitchen. Colby's face still appeared ashen; her hair hung uncommonly loose around her shoulders. She had missed a button on her blouse, and it hung crookedly. He wanted so badly to straighten out her shirt and re-button it for her, but he just clenched his fingers into fists instead.

Seconds after he sat at the table, she placed a plate of food in front of him. He stared at the veggie omelet and the dry whole grain bagel before violently pushing the plate away from him. It skidded down the table with a clatter, the bagel shooting onto the floor. Colby spun around from pouring him coffee, crying out when she sloshed the burning liquid over her hand.

He slammed his palm on the table, making her jump. "Do you call this breakfast? Can't I ever have normal white toast? And bacon? Why are you such a damn klutz? You spilled coffee all over the floor. Now fucking clean it up before it stains the floor. I'm going out for breakfast. I won't be home for dinner either."

"Mace..." she whispered, her voice shaky and breathless.

He left Colby cooling her burned fingers off under the faucet. He hadn't missed the tears filling her eyes, but he couldn't let it affect him. He just couldn't. It was for her own good. Even if she didn't know it. It had to be this way.

It had to be.

Fuck.

THE HOUSE WAS SO QUIET. Mace really hadn't come home for dinner last night. Or tonight either. He hadn't come home at all.

Colby needed to talk to him. She wanted to know what bothered him. Why he acted that way yesterday morning. Had she done something wrong?

Maybe he didn't want a woman who came with baggage. Maybe after seeing the episode with Craig and, not to mention, the PFA and horrible pictures, he realized she was more trouble than she was worth. Maybe his anger finally caught up to him, and he was pissed off about her keeping Craig a secret from him. He made it clear he wasn't happy that Martin knew about her past, that she shared personal matters with her assistant but not with Mace, her lover.

Or maybe their relationship had become too complicated too quickly for him, and he needed to step back.

Now, at only a half hour until midnight, she stood facing his closed bedroom door. She tried the knob, surprised to find it unlocked. The room was dark as she closed the door behind her. She felt her way over to the bed to turn on the lamp. The light illuminated the messy sheets, and they reminded her of the pleasure she'd found in Mace's arms. Only now, it was turning into Hell.

He had chased one hell—Craig—out of her life, only to bring in another.

For the past two days, she'd found it impossible to concentrate at work. Her stomach had been clenched into a tight ball, and she might as well not have been there at all. Though Martin had shown concern, he backed off quickly when she snapped at him.

She studied Maxi's framed picture. She missed her friend but refused to bug her and put a damper on her newly wedded bliss. Even so, she needed someone to talk to. To ask what went wrong. Maybe he'd been in miserable pain. She hoped that was it, even though she didn't want him suffering.

Colby ran a hand over the rumpled sheets. Cold. Just the opposite of all those hot nights together.

She wandered over to his dresser and picked up his cologne. When she sniffed the bottle, the recognizable scent tightened things in her lower body. She gathered his sweats off the floor and folded them, placing them on the end of his bed, wondering if he had done his physical therapy today. Maybe he would come back feeling better and everything would return to normal.

With a sigh, she drifted around the room, touching the frames hanging on the wall. Among the pictures were his high school and college diplomas. Colby stepped closer to read them; he had his BS in criminal justice.

A dark line in the wall, a slight opening, drew her attention to a tiny closet with its door ajar. Not the normal closet he hung his clothes in, she had never noticed this one before. The two-foot high door, painted the same color as the walls, had no knob or hinges to give it away.

She crossed the room but hesitated as guilt washed over her. She shouldn't be snooping, but she wanted to know more about this man. More about the man she knew so well but, honestly, hardly knew at all. He was so full of secrets, never talking about his work or past relationships. Nothing.

So, he couldn't be mad she had kept Craig a dirty little secret. He couldn't be; that wouldn't make sense. She needed to stop guessing. She just had to clear up this misunderstanding, if that's what it was, when he got home.

The little door creaked when she slowly pulled it open and peered into the dark compartment, attempting to see inside. A few boxes of files and a small file cabinet filled the tight space. Colby tugged on a drawer. All locked. She grabbed the closest banker's box and dragged it out into the light and knocked the lid off. It was stuffed full of manila folders with a name written in marker on each tab.

One thick file laid on top, like it had been recently removed and just tossed back in haste. Written in black block print was the name *Manni Spinozi*.

Spinozi. Though the name sounded familiar, she couldn't exactly place it.

She opened the file and found a picture clipped to one side of the sleeve and a profile on the man bound on the other side. She studied the photo of a dark-complexioned man, very well dressed. An obvious candid shot, he didn't appear to know this picture was being taken. She remembered hearing his name on the news but couldn't recall why.

As she scanned the profile, she heard voices from the hallway. She recognized Mace's, but the other—a woman's—she didn't know at all.

Her heart racing, she tossed the file back into the box and slapped the lid on it with shaking hands. She shoved the heavy box back into the closet and quickly shut the door. She rose to her feet as the bedroom door banged open.

Mace stopped in the doorway, his arm draped around a bleach-bottle blonde.

She stared at them in surprise, and they stared back at her. No one breathed until the blonde giggled.

"What are you doing in my room?"

Colby blinked. "I…" And blinked again, at a loss for words. Her brain didn't comprehend what she saw. "I…"

His eyes raked her, and she suddenly felt self-conscious in the oversized T-shirt she sometimes slept in. The woman who smiled up at Mace wore a short, black leather skirt and a little shiny, gold halter top. One which did not cover her breasts completely. The outfit looked a little trashy. No, very trashy, but way sexier than Colby's shapeless tee.

"Were you waiting for me like some lonely—"

Her attention went back to Mace. *Think, think, think.* "No! I…I forgot something of mine. I came in here to get it."

"Did you find it?"

She watched Mace's dangling hand brush against top of the blonde's breasts. They were hard to miss, hanging out like that. She nodded, unable to get any sound past the lump in her throat.

"Good. Now, we want to be alone." He sneered at her. "Get out."

She couldn't take her eyes off the two of them standing hip to hip in the bedroom doorway. When Mace leaned down gave the blonde a long, wet kiss on her bright red lips, Colby looked away.

"Can't you take a hint?"

She neared the couple blocking the doorway but paused to sniff the air. "Are you drunk?"

Mace let out an explosive curse, pushing the blonde aside and reaching for Colby. He grabbed her arm to pull her into the hallway. His tight grip hurt her, but she couldn't escape. He was frightening her. This wasn't the man she thought he was.

Hell, it was Craig all over again! She'd vowed she would never be in this position ever again, never allow herself to be beaten down, mentally or physically. And now—

His low, menacing words scared her even more. "You're

suffocating me, woman! I can't take it! I want you out of this house. Tomorrow."

Colby finally yanked her arm free. "Don't worry, I'll be out of here tonight."

She rushed down the hallway and into her bedroom where she flung herself on her bed and smothered her wrenching sobs in her pillow. When they subsided, she felt empty and angry. At herself.

Damn it. She had fallen. Hard, too. But there was no one to blame but herself. She told herself many times not to get involved, especially with a man like Mace. But she'd gone and done it again. And, once again, she ended up the loser.

She clenched the bedspread with shaky fingers. It was her own stupidity. She was stupid enough to...

Holy crap, she had fallen in love with this man! The one who was in his bedroom down the hall with another woman this very moment, ripping her heart out. She sniffled and grabbed a tissue to blow her nose. She needed to get a grip. She survived a rotten relationship before, she could do it again. She had to.

She would just gather her things out of her room—no, this was his room—and move into her own house. It might not be ready, but she had nowhere else to go. Ironically, she had more done than she originally planned to by this time since Mace had helped complete a lot of the work. She would make do.

Once she packed her clothes into her suitcases, she only had to get her personal items from the bathroom—which, unfortunately, sat across the hall from Mace.

As she crept down the hall, she heard giggles and groans, passionate cries.

Colby wanted to cover her ears with her hands, but she didn't. She needed to know the truth about the sneaky, low-down man. And she couldn't find a better way than listening to the man she loved have sex with another woman.

She closed the bathroom door behind her before she sobbed out loud.

~

MACE HEARD the squeal of the convertible's tires. She left.

"Okay, knock it off."

The blonde glanced up in surprise from what she was doing... which was trying to get his pants unzipped. "What's the matter, baby?"

"Nothing. I paid you to play the part. Not actually do it." He jerked away from her and pushed to his feet.

"I don't mind, honey, if you want to play a little." She reached for him with her red painted nails. "You're kind of cute."

He stepped back away from the bed and tucked his shirt back in. "I do mind."

The last thing he needed was this woman getting her claws in him since she was probably an equivalent of a petri dish. But she was the best he could find in this town; there weren't too many strip clubs to choose from.

"Oh, come on. You can't blame a girl for trying."

Mace dug into his back pocket and pulled out his wallet. He threw a fifty on the bed.

"For fifty bucks, you can get a little more than play acting." She smiled at him, licked her lips, and gave him an over-exaggerated wink.

Jesus Christ. She was not for him. At all. "No thanks, I'll call you a cab."

"Party-pooper."

He closed his eyes. Colby had called him a party-pooper once. Yeah, maybe he was. But he was in no mood to "party" with this woman. He wanted Colby. He wanted her so badly, his heart ached. She belonged in his arms. And his bed.

But now she was gone. Though, it was for the best.

Yeah, her leaving was for the best. He needed to keep telling himself that.

Fuck.

CHAPTER 13

COLBY STROLLED around her newly painted porch, enjoying the evening breeze. She surveyed the front yard. Her landscaper had done a great job. The grass was beginning to look like a real yard. The bushes were pruned and the trees cut back to allow more light around the house. Soon, little patches of flowers would pop up, giving the place some color around the trees, up the walk, around the light posts.

She sighed. It would be beautiful. Too bad she had no one to share it with.

At work, Martin had noticed her mood and even suggested she go out on a blind date. Although she refused each time, he wouldn't let up. He knew the perfect guy and what do you know? He was straight, too. Colby had to laugh at his remark, making Martin smile. He'd finally broken her sad streak. Even if just for a moment.

Eventually, she agreed to the blind date since she saw no point in just sitting around the house moping every night. It had been three weeks since she left Mace's house.

Three weeks. Three long, miserable weeks. She missed him.

Hell, she loved him. The idiot had made her go and fall in love with him. *Damn him.*

He was probably fooling around with every bimbo he could find. She had been nothing but a distraction for him. A temporary plaything. Convenient, since she lived in his home. She had cooked, cleaned, and even done his laundry. And not to mention, helped with his physical therapy. What a damned fool she was.

Once a fool, always a fool. How many times had she heard women who were abused always look for another abuser? Whether they mean to or not.

Mace might not have been an abuser, but he was definitely a user.

Now she stood here, waiting for a blind date. What was wrong with her? She should give up the male sex completely.

A silver four-door sedan pulled up the driveway. A smartly dressed man got out and gave her a slight wave.

"Robert?" Approaching him, she gave him the once-over. His brown hair wasn't nearly as dark as Mace's. He was much shorter and stockier too, but he had a nice smile.

"Hello, you must be Colby." He took her hand and brushed his lips across her knuckles. A real gentleman. "You are more beautiful than Martin said."

Heat crawled into Colby's cheeks. "Thank you."

"Are you ready?"

She nodded, giving him a forced smile. When Robert opened the car door for her, she slid in, murmuring, "Ready as I'll ever be."

MACE PACED BACK and forth in front of the restaurant, his fists clenching and unclenching at a furious pace. He paused once more to peer through the window.

What was she doing? *Fuck!* Who was that with her?

What the hell was he doing here, anyhow? Christ, he was being stupid. Not to mention, so freaking careless.

He stepped away from the window, disappearing into the darkness. He leaned against the brick building, his fists still clenched painfully as he tried to make sense of this. When he pushed her out of his bed, his house...*his life*, he hadn't expected her to fall into another man's arms so soon.

How could she be on a date with that guy? And it looked like she was enjoying herself. She kept smiling up at him even though the guy looked like such a nerd. Like a fellow scientist...He groaned.

Mace had to refrain from rushing into the restaurant and yanking her out of there. He wanted to throw her over his shoulder and carry her home. Back to him. Back to his bed.

He sucked in a deep breath, tilting his head to look up at the night sky, partly concealed by the street light. He shouldn't be here. He had to stop tailing her. This wasn't accomplishing anything, except grief on his part. And it was definitely unsafe for her. He knew better.

He was thinking with his heart and his dick, not his head.

After pushing away from the wall, he glanced in the window one last time. That's when he noticed the car. Not only was his own dumb ass reflected in the window, but so was a long black Lincoln with dark tinted windows.

He tensed. A bullet could strike him any second, and he would be caught with his pants down. Just like he followed Colby, he'd been tailed. Spinozi's men knew exactly where he was.

They knew he had followed Colby here.

They fucking knew.

Colby would be in danger, and he did it. It was all his fault.

He had to get out of there and lead them away from Colby. He couldn't risk warning her on the slight chance they hadn't realized Mace was following her. Maybe.

He could only hope.

Fighting a last look into the restaurant, Mace slipped away into the alley.

ROBERT ESCORTED Colby up the porch and to the front door where she turned to face him. "Well, thanks for a nice evening."

He cradled one of her hands in his. His felt much softer and smaller than Mace's. Not one callus, either.

"It was a wonderful evening. I hope you enjoyed it. I certainly did."

He eyed her mouth, and she realized with a start, he might try to kiss her. She tugged her hand away gently and stepped back. "Good night."

Robert looked as though he wanted to say something but refrained. Instead, he smiled at her and nodded knowingly. "Yes, good night, Colby. If you don't mind, I'd like to call you again."

She nodded slightly and watched him return to his car. She didn't unlock the front door until he drove away. She released a loud sigh.

Robert couldn't hold a candle to Mace. She really tried to like Robert tonight.

She laughed at his jokes, smiled at his compliments. Everything. She tried. But there was nothing there. Not even a hint of a spark. Damn Mace for making her want him.

And only him.

She opened the door and reached for the light switch.

"Colby," came the whisper near her ear. She yanked her hand back and squealed in surprise.

"Shh. It's me."

"Mace!" Her eyes slowly adjusted to the dark, but she could barely make out his figure in the foyer. "What the hell are you doing here? How did you get in?"

"I'm not going to play twenty questions right now. I need to talk to you."

"If you're here to beg for forgiveness—" Mace's vehement curse stopped her cold. *I guess not.* "Why can't I turn on the light?" she asked, annoyed. She needed light to make sure she hit her target when she kicked him in those cheating nuts.

"Because I don't want anyone to see I'm in the house."

"Who's going to see?" she asked, losing patience with this game he played.

"Nobody, hopefully. That's the point."

"Will you tell me what is going on?"

"Is there somewhere we can sit down?"

So, he noticed the living room was still empty of furniture. She hadn't gotten that far yet. "The stairs."

He grabbed her arm, directing her through the darkness to her stairway. "Sit."

She sat. "Mace—"

"Colby, let me speak first. This is very important. I came here to warn you."

"Warn me? About what?"

"About a case I was working on."

"Manni Spinozi." The sudden silence chilled her. She wished she could see his face.

He settled on the step beside her. "What do you know about him?" His cold tone cut her to the quick.

"Not much. I've heard he's a big mob boss. On the FBI's Ten Most Wanted list. The ATF and the DEA would also love to get a hold of him."

"Where did you hear that?"

"The news. He was mentioned in the news a few times. Is he the one who shot you?"

"No. His brother." He cursed again, savagely. "I'm sorry, Colby. I'm so sorry."

"For what?" Why couldn't she turn on the light? Not being able to read his

face drove her crazy. It scared her. She felt she was missing half of the story.

"For getting you involved."

"With you?" It was about time he apologized.

"With this. This mess."

"How—"

"Just being with me could put you in danger. If they have any idea how I feel about..." His voice drifted off. He released a long, tumultuous sigh.

"Feel about what?" she prodded.

"Hopefully, they don't know about you. I hope I got you out of my house in time."

"Out of the house," she repeated. Slowly, things became clear. "You drove

me out with that...that *woman*? You mean to tell me it was because of that guy?"

"He's reason enough. Colby, you don't know *that guy*. I do. I infiltrated his 'family.' He knows it now, and he's out for me. I can take care of myself, but it will be hard to protect you unless I keep you locked in a room."

Colby's spine stiffened. "What? I hope you're not—"

"No. Fuck no. I'm not going to. I hope I didn't do anything stupid tonight to jeopardize your safety."

"Like what?"

"Like...*Shit*. Following you on your date." The words tumbled out quickly, catching Colby by surprise. "I tried to stay away, but I failed. I wasn't going to tell you anything. I wasn't going to warn you. Damn it, I wanted to keep you uninvolved. It's risky for me to be here now as it is. But I had to warn you. I had to." It sounded as though he was trying to convince himself more than her. "I did something stupid, and you need to know."

"You followed me." It wasn't a question, more a statement of disbelief. She stood up and wandered away in the dark, feeling her way around.

"Colby, I made a mistake."

"A mistake. Am I the mistake? Was bringing the blonde bimbo home a mistake? Or are you just mad you had to admit to following me?"

In the dark, she could see he held his head in his hands, but not much more. He didn't answer her. She didn't know if she really wanted to know the answers to her questions, anyway.

"Mace, you were sloppy. Even I—what would you people call me —a *civilian* could see that. No wonder you got shot in the line of duty. Careless people get hurt." She wanted to hurt him, hurt him badly like he hurt her. Her spiteful words didn't make her feel any better. She felt worse.

"I…I'm going to bed." She brushed past him up the dark stairs. At the top of the stairs, she paused. "You know your way out."

CHAPTER 14

MACE REMAINED frozen in place while he listened to the click of her heels as she went down the hallway. Not surprisingly, a door slammed.

This hadn't gone exactly as planned. Though what had since meeting her?

He sure fucked everything up tonight, and he couldn't afford any more mistakes. She was right. He had been careless, and that same carelessness got him injured and almost cost him his career. He had to get his act together. His feelings for Colby were making him reckless, putting them both at risk.

The dead-bolt slid into place on the front door and then methodically he went around the first floor, making sure all the windows were secure. He would call an alarm company in the morning.

After fighting the temptation to run up the stairs and into her arms at least a half dozen times, he slipped out the back of the house a few minutes later, making sure the door was locked behind him.

He drove home, more determined than ever to extract himself from Colby's life.

The only way Mace knew how to get Spinozi's men away from

her, short of killing them all—impossible, even for him—was to leave town. They would follow him, like good little goons do. And there was no doubt he was being followed. Mace knew they were waiting for the right moment to swoop in.

He also knew they wouldn't make him a quick, easy hit. Spinozi wanted him to suffer.

He was a sitting duck if he stayed in his house. The hit proved they knew his real name and where he lived. He needed to get ghost. Now.

Back at the house, he threw a few things in his bag. He needed to get in touch with his boss for a new assignment.

He would no longer be Macen Jeffrey Walker, but somebody else. Joe Schmoe, if need be. It would be a few more years before Mace Walker showed up again, if ever.

Of course, he would warn Maxi before coming back from her trip. He'd get a real estate agency to sell the house for him. He, and even Maxi, could never live here again safely.

His biggest regret was not having the chance to see or speak to his sister. He would have to find a way to contact her in the future. When, and if, it was ever safe. With her new married name, Spinozi and his gang might not realize they were even related. And he'd like to keep it that way.

The home phone rang, jerking him out of his thoughts. *Fuck!* Why hadn't he smashed them all yet?

When he reluctantly lifted the receiver to his ear, he immediately heard uncontrollable sobbing on the other end. This wasn't Colby just upset with him about tonight. *Christ.* He broke out in a cold sweat and sank to the floor, clutching the phone so tightly, his knuckles turned white.

A gruff voice ordered, "Say something, you fuckin' bitch!" The sobbing became louder. "Damn you, say something!"

Mace heard a loud slap followed by silence. Then finally, murmured curses in the background.

"Son of a bitch," Mace muttered. "Son of a bitch! You fucking hurt her and—"

Suddenly, laughter came over the line, making Mace's spine stiffen. "What? What will you do, call the cops, Rico? I mean Macen Walker. Your name isn't Rico, is it?"

He didn't answer. He couldn't. He would never tell his secrets. Never. Even if it meant death. But Colby hadn't taken the oath. She didn't deserve to die. "Where are you?" Mace ground out.

"Aah. In a pretty yellow kitchen. One freshly painted. It's a shame this house will light up like fireworks soon, taking your little lover girl. Is she good, Rico? In bed, I mean."

Mace slammed down the phone. He grabbed his gun and tucked it into the back of his waistband as he ran out of the house.

MACE'S TRUCK skidded to a stop nearly a block away from the house. It hadn't even been an hour since he'd been there earlier. Not one freaking hour! He should have stayed.

No, he should have stayed away.

He scrambled out of the truck cab and moved quickly down the sidewalk, sticking close to the shrubs, his gun in hand. Just as he reached the corner of her driveway and the shrubbery, he stopped and took a deep breath. *Slow down and think.* He couldn't just rush in; he'd get them both killed.

Spinozi's men wanted him. That was the game. Colby was only the bait. He had to get in there without getting her killed. They would think nothing of taking her life. Hell, they might do it just for the sport of it. He stepped away from the shrubs into the dark driveway, determined to remain undetected until the last second.

The explosive red hot flash blinded him, the impact knocking him off his feet. Landing hard on his back, he found himself unable to breathe, no oxygen left in his lungs. His gun had flown out of his hand and skidded down the pavement.

He lay there for a second, gasping, fighting for breath. Finally, he pushed himself to his knees. Using both hands on the ground for leverage, he unfolded his body until he stood. But seeing the devastation, he struggled to keep his feet underneath him.

The house was gone. Totally fucking gone. Flames shot up from the rubble. Only burning splinters of wood remained of the house Colby had loved so much.

The house was completely gone. *Colby.*

He sank to his knees, digging his fingers into his hair and pulling, trying to relieve the agony clawing the inside of his head. He screamed, no sound escaping, until he ran out of air and dropped his head into his hands.

The heat from the burning timbers reminded him of what he had to do. Who he was.

Damn them. Damn them all to mighty hell. They were going to die. All of them. Every single one of those motherfuckers.

Hands grabbed him from behind—on his arms, around his neck. He tried to jerk away. He looked for his gun. Outnumbered, his struggling got him nowhere. Then someone kicked him in the head from behind.

The world went black.

MOANING. Louder now. Mace shook his head to clear it but doing so only brought a shard of pain.

He struggled to open his swollen eyes. Through the slits, he could barely see the metal chair he was tied to. Warm liquid oozed down his forehead, trickling into his eye. His tongue seemed twice its normal size, and his mouth felt stuffed with cotton.

Blood-soaked cotton.

Doing a mental body check, the intense pain in his side made him wonder if they'd broken his ribs. The sting at the back of his head and his stiff hair most likely meant he had a nasty gash. His face was dripping with blood, some of it crusting already, and he couldn't even feel one side. Maybe it was better that way. He tried to lick his dry, cracked lips, but it was impossible. His tongue was cut, probably from his own teeth.

He scoped out the area as best as he could with his limited vision. Whoever had him here sat behind him talking quietly. Mace tried to make out what they were saying through the ringing in his right ear. He turned his head slightly, not enough to draw attention to him, so his good ear could pick up the conversation.

"He'll be here soon. He wants us to wait until he's here. He wants to watch the man who killed his brother die."

"We better be gettin' that damn prize money."

"We'll get it. He's good for it."

The loud moan again. He turned his head a fraction toward the sound and damned his vision when it blurred for a moment.

Fuck.

Colby. She was alive.

All the oxygen left him, but his relief was short-lived. They were in a bad, bad situation. One he doubted he could get them out of. They were fucked. Fucked was putting it mildly, knowing Spinozi's men.

She sat bound to another metal chair across, but at an angle, from him. Duct tape sealed her mouth. Her face, distorted on one side from swelling, was already turning purple. Her head hung, like it was too much effort for her to lift it. That or she was blessedly unconscious. He could only hope.

"Colby!" he yelled before he could stop himself. He just had to know if she was…all right. Stupid but true.

Her head lifted slightly and, as she noticed him, her hollowed eyes widened in surprise and then grief.

Mace heard a scuffle of feet before a deep voice right behind him said, "Shut up!"

He managed to get "Fuck you" out before everything went black again when something hard was rudely introduced to the back of his head.

~

THE WORLD CLEARED AGAIN, somewhat, when a hand slapped his face. And slapped again.

"Wake up! Wake up, you worthless piece of shit!"

The throbbing in his head pounded even harder as he opened his eyes and the lights temporarily blinded him. "Christ," he moaned.

"No one asked you to speak. At least, not until you're spoken to." The man himself stood in front of him. Shit couldn't get any deeper than right at that moment. "Who are you working for?" Spinozi asked.

"No one."

"You're gonna be loyal to the end, are you? We'll see about that." Spinozi nodded to the goons behind Mace. "Cut off his left pant leg. I want to see the damage my brother did before this asshole killed him."

One of Mace's captors took a knife to his jeans, exposing his mangled thigh.

"I'm impressed you still have use of this leg, *Macen Walker*. We might have to do something about that. Does it hurt?"

Mace said nothing; instead he glanced over at Colby. Now fully conscious, she watched what was going on with wide eyes. She looked very, very afraid. He didn't blame her. He wasn't feeling too brave himself.

He was going to die, and he knew it. It didn't matter what he said tonight, he would still die. The only thing which could change was how long it would take. He had a feeling they might take their time.

Spinozi put the heel of his shoe on Mace's exposed thigh and twisted it back and forth, as if grinding out a cigarette. He gritted his teeth, which caused more pain in his swollen jaw. He would not react. He would not.

He. Would. Not...ever...give that satisfaction to the bastard.

Mace struggled to keep eye contact with Colby. Even with the distance between them, he couldn't mistake the tears trickling from the corners of her eyes. She tried to say something, but the tape muffled her voice. She yanked at her ties, but it was useless. Even if she could get loose, what could she do?

Not satisfied with Mace's response, Spinozi cursed and stopped. He turned to study Colby. Realizing his worst fear, Mace knew Spinozi would use her against him. The fat bastard would use her to break him down. Mace would rather have the bastard torture him forever than touch her even once.

"I'm assuming she was more beautiful before my men got to her, hmm? It's a shame to mess up a pretty face like hers," Spinozi said with a slight upturn to his mouth. He stepped over to Colby but made sure he didn't block Mace's view. Spinozi ran a finger down her cheek, smearing her fresh tears with the dried blood already there. "Look, Walker, she's crying for you." He laughed, causing Colby to jerk against her bindings. "She's got a nice little body, doesn't she? Would you mind sharing her with my men?"

Mace tensed and ground out, "You fucking touch her and—"

Spinozi and his men laughed. The laughter boomed through the large, empty warehouse, echoing back to him and emphasizing what he already knew. He'd fucked up. He should have kept his mouth shut. What he'd said had been stupid. He couldn't follow through on any threats. He could do absolutely nothing but watch whatever they did to Colby. Now he actually wished she was dead. She'd be better off dead than tortured.

Spinozi grabbed Colby's blouse and ripped it open, the buttons flying off in different directions. The laughter quickly died around him. His men knew what would be next. He held out his hand for the knife. When he got it, he sliced open her bra, exposing her breasts. A thin line of blood appeared where the knife nicked her sternum. By accident? Nothing Spinozi did was an accident.

Colby squeezed her eyes closed. Her humiliation overwhelmed him, only frustrating him more.

"How would it be to watch your lover being fucked by six men in front of you, huh?" Spinozi wore a wicked grin. "You just might enjoy it. Both of you. Is she sweet, Walker? Have you tasted her honey?"

The crime boss walked behind Colby and placed a hand on her shoulder. A gun appeared in the other, and he pressed it to her temple. "Maybe you'd rather see her brains splattered all over you." Spinozi bent down and whispered something into her ear. The duct tape covering her mouth puffed out then sucked in as her breathing became faster, frantic.

Mace tugged against the ropes binding his hands until he felt a trickle of blood run down his fingers. Useless. "Damn you! If you're going to kill her, just do it. She knows nothing; she's got nothing to do with this! Don't torture her for nothing!"

Spinozi lifted a dark eyebrow. "Are you begging for her life?"

"You want me, you've got me. Torture me if you're going to torture anybody."

"There's no *if* about it."

"So torture me, you shit-for-brains, not her!"

Mace's attempt to piss Spinozi off seemed to work. The man left Colby to step closer to him, jamming the gun against Mace's lips. "Watch your mouth, before I blow it right off your face!"

"Do it," he goaded between pressed lips.

"It's not going to be that easy, Walker. No way. I'm not in a rush, and you and your girlfriend have nowhere else to go."

Colby squeezed her eyes tight. Any moment, she would wake up and this would all be a bad nightmare. She had seen scenes like this in the movies. This does not happen in real life.

This could not be happening.

But it was.

She opened her eyes when she heard a noise she didn't even want to guess at. Bile threatened to rise up into her throat.

The half-dozen men behind Mace kept staring her bare breasts. The sick, wicked grins on their faces didn't change when they went back to watching Mace suffer. She couldn't figure out which excited them more. But her exposed chest was the least of her worries.

Mace was in serious trouble. They were both going to die. But not without suffering first. She was sure of it. How the hell could she help him or herself? Even if she could free herself, she had no idea where they were. A garage or warehouse, maybe. It could be in another state or even another country. She didn't know how long she'd been passed out before waking up tied to this damn metal chair.

Colby watched the violence continue against Mace through a haze. She didn't know how long it lasted. An hour. Two? It could have been twenty minutes, for all she knew.

She lost track of time. Pinning her eyes shut against the horror, she slowly rocked back and forth, as far as the bindings would allow.

Too many questions went unanswered. The only answers Spinozi got for his needling were the slight sounds of pain occasionally slipping from Mace's lips. They beat him, stabbed him, sliced and burned. Again and again. *No man could take this*, she thought wildly. Mace either refused to, or could not, answer the questions they shouted at him.

She knew, even if he answered, they wouldn't give them mercy, anyway. She wasn't stupid.

"Now for the best part of the night," Spinozi announced with a great flourish. "Untie his right hand. Leave the other bound."

She heard a scuffle and then a groan as one of Mace's hands became free. "Take it," Spinozi ordered. "Take it!"

Colby didn't want to look, but she couldn't help it. Mace, his face swollen almost beyond recognition, slowly reached out to take the handgun.

Shoot the bastard, Mace! Shoot that fat bastard!

"Point it at her."

"Fuck you." The words were no more than a pained whisper. His voice unrecognizable. Not much remained of the man she knew. And loved.

Spinozi put a knife to his ear and drew blood. "Point it at her. It's easier to kill her than to watch me slice off her luscious body parts while she's awake. Isn't it, *Rico?*"

Mace raised the gun, his hand shaking. The six men stationed behind him had drawn their guns too. Half pointed at her, half at Mace. They were doomed either way.

"Shoot her. Shoot her now!"

Mace stuck the gun to his own temple instead. He wouldn't do that. It had to be a ploy.

"Stupid man," Spinozi growled. He circled Mace. "Will you leave her alone with us, then? Pull the damn trigger, you coward. Do it!"

Colby watched his fingers tighten on the gun and his finger slide in front of the trigger. He wouldn't desert her like that. He wouldn't.

Mace met her eyes. But she saw nothing but an empty shadow of his former self. Colby wanted to scream, but the damn tape kept her mouth shut. She wanted to tell him to stop. To beg him not to pull the trigger.

"I love you," he mouthed.

Colby squeezed her eyes shut. Fine time to tell her now—when they were about to die. She fought back the hysterical laughter bubbling up from her throat. She couldn't watch. She couldn't. God, she loved him. She loved him.

She loved him.

But he was going to die.

The gun exploded, and Colby jumped, her ears rang painfully. It was over. Now it was her turn.

The ringing in her ears wouldn't go away. Neither could she open her eyes. They burned with tears and smoke and hatred. She didn't want to see the gun pointed at her. She couldn't hear anything, but after a few moments, she felt the body heat of someone near her. The duct tape was ripped off her mouth. The stinging pain couldn't compare to the suffering in her heart.

Colby opened her eyes to see men swarming around her. They

were wearing dark blue wind jackets and baseball-type caps with ATF and FBI on them in big yellow letters.

They were too late. Too late!

Someone cut her ropes. The sudden circulation to her feet and hands caused a stinging sensation. An awful prickly pain. But the pain of knowing Mace was dead was worse.

Her hearing still must have been muted from the gunshots because it took the dark-haired man in front of her a couple times before she could make out his words. "Ma'am. Here, put this on."

Colby tried to reach out for the offered jacket, but her arms refused to move. "I can't." Her raw voice sounded hoarse, and she tried to clear her throat.

The agent helped insert her arms into the sleeves, and he snapped the jacket closed, covering her nakedness. She wanted to stand, but her legs shook so badly, she tried twice before the man lifted her up. Though grateful for his help, she couldn't say thank you, for if she opened her mouth again, she would wail uncontrollably, and they would have to sedate her. Or put her in a strait jacket.

From outside the building, she finally heard the sirens. She hadn't noticed them earlier due to her hearing loss. But those high-pitched wails sounded good to her now.

She looked around to see the officers dragging Spinozi's men out of the door, shackled like the animals they were. She wished she had her Glock so she could shoot every one of them between the eyes. She spotted the gun in the agent's holster. It was within reach.

He must have noticed her gaze, since he turned his hip away from her and said, "The ambulance is here, ma'am. Do you think you can walk? I'll help you."

Taking her arm, he supported her while she walked out the door, careful to keep her on his left side, away from his weapon.

"There's only one ambulance left, ma'am. So, you'll have to hitch a ride." The man gave her a gentle smile as he handed her over to the EMTs, who helped her climb into the back of the ambulance.

"Sit here," one of them said, pointing to a seat next to the gurney.

She sat, in a daze, and looked to see who she rode with. If it was Spinozi, she'd kill him right now, before they could get to the hospital. She didn't need the agent's gun; she'd kill him with her bare hands. "My God..." she whispered. She turned to the EMT next to her. "Is he alive?"

"Yes. He's been in and out of consciousness. Look."

Colby leaned forward. Mace. He hadn't shot himself. Those deafening gunshots must have all come from the agents' guns.

He *was* alive. But— "Is he all right?"

"He's in a critical condition."

Mace slowly lifted a hand to Colby's face. He couldn't quite reach, so she leaned closer, crying out with disbelief when he touched her skin. His bottom lip was split and blood trickled from his mouth, but he tried to speak.

She leaned even closer until her ear was a breath away. "What?"

"Will you marry me?"

She was hearing things. Why would he ask her that? Here, now? While he fought for his life?

The EMT pulled her back. "Ma'am, please. Sit back, give us some room to work."

Colby sat back. And wept.

EPILOGUE

"Why won't they let me see him?" Colby yelled to no one in particular while she paced the hospital hallway. Not only frustrated and angry, she was plain spitting mad. She had waited for six hours— time enough for doctors to clean her up, stitch her up, and officially release her—and now they refused to let her see Mace.

"Probably because you aren't family."

She spun toward the voice. "Who are you?"

The man was short, bald, and stocky but wore a well-fitted, deep blue suit and dark glasses. Who wore sunglasses inside?

"I can't tell you who I am. Just think of me as a concerned citizen."

Concerned citizen. Right. She damn well knew he was Mace's boss. She was sick of this secret squirrel shit which landed them both in the hospital. "Why won't they let me in to see him? I'm his fiancée!" Maybe he had enough influence to get her into Mace's room.

The man raised an eyebrow. "Oh?"

Then Colby swore she heard, "The SOB finally got the best of me," under his breath. Before she could question him on it, he continued louder, "Well, Ms. Parks, congratulations. And for your wedding present, I'd like to give you Mace's walking papers."

He handed her a thick manila envelope. Though free of writing on the outside, a federal government seal marked one corner. She tore her eyes away from the official-looking envelope to catch her reflection in his sunglasses. "Walking papers?"

"Yes, Agent Walker is officially retired as of midnight tonight."

Colby sank down in a chair, staring at the packet. She flipped it over in her hands a couple times before saying, "Retired? Honorably, I assume."

The man laughed. "There are no honors in his line of work, Ms. Parks. Just be glad we got there in time to keep him alive."

She picked at the sealed edge of the envelope. She glanced up. "May I?" He gave a slight incline to his head, enough of an answer for her to tear the flap open. As she slid the paperwork out she asked, "How did you know where we were?"

She started to scan the cover letter when she realized he hadn't answered her. Colby looked up. He was gone. If it wasn't for the paperwork she held in her hands, she would have thought she imagined him.

She finished scanning the letter before flipping through the rest of the package which included details of his pension, retirement benefits, and a lot of legalese.

A nurse quietly approached her. "Ms. Parks, you may see him now."

"What? I thought—"

"Mr. Smith explained your situation, and we realized we'd been mistaken."

Colby silently thanked *Mr. Smith* as she rushed past the nurse and raced down the hallway. She couldn't push the door open fast enough to enter Mace's room.

His head was cushioned by a pillow, his upper body held in an upright position due to the medical bed. Ugly black stitches crisscrossed his face, one ear, his arm...She stopped searching. There were too many sutured areas to count. He reminded her of Frankenstein, though not as scary. His eyes were closed, and his breathing steady. An IV protruded from his left arm, and he had some sort of machine hooked to him, beeping every second or so.

She dragged one of the blocky hospital room chairs next to his bed and perched on the edge. When she reached out for his right hand, the one unencumbered with tubes, he met her halfway. His warm, long fingers enveloped hers. Her eyes flicked back to his face, and he watched her through unreadable swollen, purple eyes. He gave her fingers a slight squeeze.

Without letting go of her lifeline, she placed the packet of papers gently on his chest. He lifted his head off the pillow a little, asking "What's that?" through puffy, bruised lips.

"Your tour of duty is officially over. You're retired."

When he didn't respond, she didn't know if it was a good or a bad thing. He couldn't want to continue getting shot and beaten up. How much could a body take? After tonight, she couldn't take any more. She didn't want to say, "It's me or your career." She wouldn't do that to him, but she couldn't stand by and worry about him. Or worse, lose him for good.

"Good. Now I can concentrate on other things."

Colby released her breath, not even realizing she held it while waiting for his response. He would let his job go. "What other things?"

"Building you a new home. Somewhere far away from here. Somewhere safe." His words came slowly, and it took him effort to get them out, but she understood every one of them. He gripped her hand harder. "I'm sorry your house was destroyed, Colby."

"I know." She smiled softly. "I can replace a house. I can't replace you."

He gave her a gentle tug, and she slid over to the edge of the hospital bed, careful not to jar him too much. "I know how much it meant to you, what a haven it was for you."

"You're all I need now." She brushed a finger lightly down his bruised, broken features. She laid her head on his chest, feeling it rise and fall softly with his steady breathing. "I love you, Mace."

The movement of his chest hesitated under her cheek, and a moment later, it surged and continued on with its soothing rhythm. He brushed her hair away from her face with his free hand. "How soon can I get out of this place? I'm sick of hospitals."

"Soon," she answered, but truthfully, she didn't know. He had a lot of healing to do before he could ever build their home. *Their home.*

"Where do you want to go?" he asked.

"Go?"

"Yes, where do you want to build our new house and our new life?" he clarified.

"Anywhere, Mace. Anywhere you go, I'll follow."

He chuckled softly then groaned in pain. "No, I think you've got it backward. I'll follow you. To the ends of the Earth if necessary."

Colby sighed as he tightened his fingers around hers. He lifted them to his mouth and pressed them ever so lightly to his lips.

She moved to lean her cheek against his, careful not to hurt him. She needed him, needed to feel him against her. She loved him and never wanted to let him go.

"You never answered my question," he murmured into her ear. Question. What question?

Oh.

"Yes." She laughed through her tears. "Yes, yes, yes!"

**Turn the page to read the first chapter of
Down & Dirty: Zak (Dirty Angels MC, bk 1)**

Sign up for Jeanne's newsletter to learn about her upcoming releases, sales and more! http://www.jeannestjames.com/newslettersignup

ABOUT DOWN & DIRTY: ZAK (DIRTY ANGELS MC, BK 1)

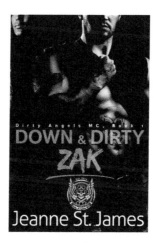

Welcome to Shadow Valley where the Dirty Angels MC rules. Get ready to get Down & Dirty because this is Zak's story...

After spending the last ten years in prison, Zak, former DAMC president, has a few priorities: to reconnect with his "brothers," to get drunk, and to get laid. Not necessarily in that order. When he spots a stunning woman in the clubhouse and mistakes her for one of the club's strippers, those priorities get a bit skewed.

Sophie has no idea what happened to her life. One minute she's totally focused on building her bakery business, and the next? She's delivering a cake to the Dirty Angels motorcycle club's "homecoming" celebration for a member who just got out of prison. Little does she know baking that cake will change the rest of her life, not to mention, make her a target for a rival MC. Normally, Sophie wouldn't be caught dead with a man like Zak, a tattooed, ex-con, badass biker.

When a decades old territory war threatens to rip them apart, Zak will do anything to keep Sophie, his club, and the town safe. But being from two different worlds, the threat they're under may not be worth the risk.

Turn the page to read Chapter One!

DOWN & DIRTY: ZAK - CHAPTER ONE

A HIGH-PITCHED BUZZ SOUNDED. The magnetic door latch released and with a violent push, Zak stepped out into the sunlight.

Not even six feet from the building, he stopped, closed his eyes, flared his nostrils and inhaled a deep breath.

Smelled like freedom.

He opened his eyes, spun on his heels and raised his arms to give the double middle finger salute to the guards watching him on the cameras. He threw his head back and laughed.

Fuck them all.

His breath condensed in the frigid air and he wore no jacket but he didn't care.

Life. Was. Good.

A horn honked and he turned to see who it was. Though, it wasn't who he'd hoped, he wouldn't gripe about it. A brother was a brother, whether blood or not.

He picked up the small bag of personal items from where he dropped it in his haste to flip the guards the bird and jogged to the curb where his chariot awaited.

Diesel tossed him his leather cut, as well as a hooded sweatshirt.

After pulling the sweatshirt over his T, he raised his colors to his nose and inhaled.

Yeah. His vest smelled like leather, smoke, booze and pussy. Best combination in the world.

The patch was dirty and worn but still made a clear statement. He was a fucking Dirty Angel and after ten years in the joint, that still hadn't changed.

This was his homecoming. And it would be his last one because he swore to himself he would never go into that concrete box again.

Never.

Diesel, the club's "Enforcer," wore a huge grin when they clasped hands and bumped chests. "Good to see you, brother."

The man's smile was infectious. "Same, brother. Been too fuckin' long." He jabbed a finger at the Sergeant at Arms patch on the man's cut. "I see nothin's changed. Still bustin' heads?"

Diesel only laughed and moved around the hood of the car to the driver's side.

Zak yanked open the door of the classic Pontiac GTO—Diesel's baby after his bike—and slid onto the seat, holding his vest on his lap like it was precious. Before climbing in, Diesel shrugged out of his, turned it inside out and slipped it back over his shoulders.

You never wore your colors when riding in a "cage," and if you did, you turned your colors in. Because DAMC was a damn bike club, not a car club. That was a lesson not to be forgotten. Zak smiled at the memory of kicking some prospect's ass for disrespecting the club by wearing his vest colors out while in a car.

Good times.

As Diesel pulled away from the parking lot, the larger man's head swiveled to study him, but Zak wasn't in the mood to talk about his time inside so he said, "Let's get the fuck outta here."

"Sounds like a plan. Need to get to church anyway, everyone's gettin' together for your homecomin' celebration."

Zak glanced at him in surprise. "Yeah?"

"Fuck yeah. Want to welcome home our President."

Zak shook his head and frowned. "I'm no longer President, D. Even I'm aware of that."

Diesel grunted, then said, "That'll change," and turned the key.

The throaty roar of the big block engine was music to Zak's ears. He couldn't wait to get the power of his bike between his thighs again. He'd missed it.

He'd missed the open road.

He'd missed doing shit on his timetable and not the warden's.

Even so, he hadn't missed being the club president and didn't know if he even wanted the hassle anymore. He wanted to enjoy his newly found freedom for a while. And being constantly saddled with club business choked that freedom.

But as his gaze slid to Diesel, he didn't think the time was right to talk about it.

They had a party to go to.

Beer to drink.

He needed to reconnect with his brothers.

And, almost as important, he needed to fuck some pussy. Because ten years was way too long to go without.

First order of business back at the club would be to make his rounds. Second was to drain his clogged pipes.

And if it took more than one woman to do it? So be it.

When Diesel pulled the GTO through the gate into the rear parking lot of the clubhouse, a sense of relief overcame Zak. He breathed easier and felt himself automatically settling back into the old ways. He was home. Really fucking home.

He'd noticed there were no bikes or cars parked out front on the public side of the bar, The Iron Horse Roadhouse. Hawk must have shut the bar down so everyone could attend the pig roast, which would be held out back, the private side of the club bar.

"We got the girls to clean out one of the larger rooms upstairs so you got somewhere to crash tonight. Stay until you get yourself settled."

Zak didn't answer, he only nodded, amazed at the sight of how packed the back lot was with vehicles.

Large turnout.

Anxiety crept through him, his stomach churning a bit. He'd been gone a long time. A whole fucking decade. Things looked the same so far, but he knew there had been changes. Hopefully for the better.

Club life hadn't stood still waiting for Zak to do his time. His fingers fisted in his vest as it laid on his lap.

Diesel parked directly in front of the back entrance to the clubhouse—it was almost as if the spot had been reserved for him—and shut the car off, not moving to get out.

Zak didn't, either. Instead, he rolled his gaze up to read the sign over the grey steel-metal door.

Dirty Angels MC.

Under that, in smaller letters… *Down & Dirty 'til Dead.*

His nostrils flared as he sucked in oxygen.

This was his family. They would welcome him home with open arms.

Well, *they* would.

His dad and brother… maybe not so much.

He mentally shook that problem out of his head and shot a look at Diesel before pushing the door open and unfolding from the passenger seat. As soon as he was on his feet, he shrugged his vest over his shoulders.

That was more like it. *Now* he was home.

He glanced down to where the rectangular patch was missing, where it had been ripped free from the leather, just a few stray threads left behind as a reminder.

He was no longer president. Someone else wore that patch now.

More power to Pierce for taking on the headache.

Though, some of the brothers weren't thrilled with Pierce taking the head of the table. Even though they were all brothers at heart,

Pierce didn't come from either bloodline of the two club founders, Doc and Bear.

And Pierce didn't always agree with all of the club's business staying on the upside, staying legit. He tended to lean toward the old ways.

But the old ways had gotten way too many of them locked up. And when a brother was doing time, that meant less money in the coffers. One less member paying dues, one less member working in the businesses.

And that was not good. Not good for the club in general. Not good for the brothers who remained on the outside because they had to step up to fill in the financial gaps.

"You just gonna stand there, or you gonna take your ass inside?" Diesel prodded, making Zak shake himself mentally to get himself out of his head, his thoughts.

With a smile to his brother, he kissed the tips of his fingers then leapt straight up, tagging the club's entryway sign with his hand.

Good to be home.

Diesel laughed, yanked open the door, and shoved Zak past the threshold into the dim interior.

And then the sound was deafening. The hooting, the hollering, the cat calls, the whistles, and "fuck yeah's," as Zak parted the crowd like the Red Sea. The common area was packed. Familiar faces became a blur as he fought his way through the back pats, shoulder bumps, forearms clasps. His face began to ache from the smile he wore; it couldn't get any bigger, any wider.

He pushed his way to the club's private bar and stared at Hawk stationed behind it. The big man had his thick arms crossed over his chest and a serious expression on his face. He looked the same as Zak remembered, just ten years older. A few lines at the corners of his dark brown eyes, his dark hair in a short Mohawk. That hadn't changed, either. Both sides of his head shaved, his bare scalp sporting tattoos.

His right-hand man.

Or used to be, anyway. Zak's gaze dropped to the man's rectangular patch and was pleased to see the man was still VP.

But Zak knew that. He had been kept up to date for the most part during his stint at the State Correctional Institution in Fayette county. Most of the brothers had taken turns visiting when they could. Not that Zak expected them to, but it was good when they did.

It took everything in his power not to leap over the bar and grab the man only two years his senior into a bear hug. No matter what shit went down, Hawk always had his back.

Through thick and thin. Maybe not true brothers, but brothers all the same.

"Still as ugly as ever, chicken hawk," Zak growled at him. "Bet your hair is stiffer than your dick ever gets."

"You give me limp dick just thinking about how many salads you tossed in the joint."

Zak realized how quiet the room became around them. All eyes on them.

"What's a man gotta do to get a damn drink 'round here?"

Hawk grabbed his junk. "Suck my cock. Probably good at doin' that now. Probably a pro."

"Fucker," Zak grumbled, struggling to keep a straight face.

Izzy walked behind the bar and in between the two men having a stare down. "Boys. Just kiss and get it over with. And then get the man a damn drink."

Zak's eyes slid to Isabella. "Damn, Izzy, you're lookin' good."

"Anything with a pussy probably looks good to you right now. But," she put both palms on the bar and leaned toward Zak, "it helped that I got rid of that dead weight." She slapped a shot glass in front of him and cocked an eyebrow.

"Jack."

Izzy nodded then turned to grab the Jack Daniels from the shelf behind the bar. "Call me Bella, Zak. I'm trying to erase anything that reminds me of that rat bastard." She poured him a double.

He raised the glass up to her in a salute. "Here's to freedom. For both of us." Then downed the whiskey. The burn down his throat felt good. Real. A reminder that he was now free and needed to keep it that way.

"Amen to that," she muttered.

But she did look good. Her wavy, long dark brown hair went past the middle of her back. Her dark brown eyes looked guarded, as they should with the shit she went through with her husband—now ex. Even though it was chilly out, she wore a tight black tank top with the letters DAMC over her ample breasts with her pink bra straps showing. A wide black leather belt cinched her narrow waist, and her hips... damn, they'd widened out perfectly. Grab worthy, *hang on tight as she's bucking wild on your lap* worthy.

But even so, he wouldn't fuck her with a ten-foot pole. And one reason was standing directly behind her, watching him check her out. The other reason sidled up next to him. Diesel. Both men were brothers for real. And both men were her cousins who now kept a close eye on her. *Very* close. And he certainly didn't need a double ass-kicking fresh out of the joint.

"Know it's been ten years, but don't even think about it," Diesel muttered near his ear.

Zak lifted both palms in surrender. "Wouldn't even go there."

"Good."

They seemed to be more protective of her now than ever. And with good reason. He had heard what her ex had done to her. And he understood them getting their hackles up when a male showed interest. Though, she worked at The Iron Horse and he couldn't imagine she didn't get hit on a lot. Her curves had matured over the last ten years and he had to admit she was drop-dead gorgeous. He wondered how many asses Hawk and Diesel thumped because of that.

Izzy shifted down the bar to talk to someone else and Hawk stepped back up, pouring him another double then pouring one for

Diesel and himself. They clinked shot glasses then downed them in one swallow.

Zak slapped the glass down on the bar top and got serious. "Anyone see my dad or Axel?"

He didn't miss when Diesel and Hawk's eyes met briefly, a silent message, then their gaze broke and went back to him.

"See 'em 'round town, but haven't had any real run-ins with 'em."

"Guess they won't be here tonight," Zak said softly, trying to fight the disappointment, but having a hard time keeping it from his voice.

"You know how it is with those fuckin' cops, Z," Jag said, walking up behind him and pounding him a welcome on the back. "They stick with their own. They don't wanna get dirt under their nails by fraternizin' with us."

Zak turned to his cousin, and they clasped hands as if they were about to arm wrestle and then bumped shoulders.

Jag muttered, "Fuck that," and wrapped his beefy arms around Zak and squeezed him tight.

Zak thought he spotted a tear in his blood relative and the club Road Captain's eye.

Nah. Couldn't have been.

Dirty Angels never cried. Even when they did.

And if they did, no one noticed or talked about it. Ever.

One time a prospect made fun of a patched member who got emotional and he ended up disappearing. Just like that.

Poof.

But then that was in the old days.

Even a hard-assed MC member shed some tears once in a while. But, again, somehow no one ever noticed.

"Uncle Mitch and your brother have been scarce. When the pigs show up here, for whatever reason they feel's 'necessary,' they usually send anyone but them. And from what Dad says, they've circled the wagons 'round Jayde since she's come home from college. They don't want her gettin' anywhere near the club or any of us dirty fuckers."

"With good reason," Zak joked. Or tried to. He missed his little sister, too. The last time he saw her she was around fourteen years old. His mother and she had sat in the back of the courtroom for his sentencing and once it was over, he turned to look at them and they were gone. Disappeared. It probably had been too much for them.

So, he didn't blame them. And he tried not to take it to heart that no one from his immediate family had ever visited him once while he was at Fayette. He understood their desire to keep their lives separate.

Though, his grandfather would have been pissed if he'd still been alive. The club had been his grandfather's heart and soul.

Fuck.

He was supposed to be celebrating, not getting morose.

Zak cleared the thick out of his throat and said, "Proud of you for gettin' voted in as Road Captain."

Jag dropped his head, breaking eye contact, and murmured, "Nah, it was nothin'. Someone had to step up."

"I'm glad it was you."

Suddenly, he was body slammed from the back. Then slammed again. He turned to see Ace, Diesel and Hawk's father, and Dex, their cousin and Izzy's brother.

"Holy fuck, boy, you don't look worse for wear," Ace boomed. "C'mere, you fucker."

Ace pulled Zak into his arms and squeezed tight, making it hard for Zak to breathe, but before he let go, he murmured in his ear, "Thank fuck you're out. Gotta get this club back on track."

Zak schooled the surprise from his face before he turned to Dex, who only smiled at him and said, "Fuckin' A, brother. You've been greatly missed."

Zak's lips thinned and he nodded. The back of his throat tickled with unshed tears and he blinked away any evidence of weakness.

To cover up his emotions, he pointed at Ace's patch which read Treasurer, and shouted, "You assholes still trust this guy with our money?"

Laughter surrounded him. Then he spun on Dex and pointed to his patch. "Secretary? Who taught Dex how to read an' write?"

Dex laughed, pounded him on the back and grabbed the shot glass Izzy shoved at him. He lifted it toward Zak in salute and then downed it.

Ace grabbed Zak's arm and pulled him over to the side, leaning in. "Left a message on your father's phone to let him know you were comin' home today." Ace shook his head, his face dropping. "Sorry, son. Didn't even get a text back."

"To be expected," Zak said, then gave him a reassuring half smile. "Thanks for tryin', though."

Then a booming voice rose from out of the crowd. "Get the fuck outta my way."

Grizz.

Goddamn. It was going to get even harder to hide his emotions once that old man got to him. The crowd of onlookers let him through and he stopped about five feet from Zak, inspecting him from head to toe.

"You don't look worse for wear," Grizz echoed Ace.

"Hell, no," Zak answered. "Was like Club Fed in there. Couldn't ask for a better vacation."

"Boy, come give this ol' man a bear hug." And with that, he opened his thick arms wide and Zak, with a smile, stepped into them. "Fuckin' A," Grizzly mumbled and sniffed.

"Don't you start," Zak warned softly. "You start an' I'm a goner."

Grizz nodded and then shoved Zak away from him. Zak caught his balance before facing the older man who was like a grandfather to him. Hell, like a grandfather to most of the members of the club. He'd been around forever. Zak couldn't remember this club without him. His beard was longer, bushier, and definitely greyer than the day Zak got locked up. But his light blue eyes twinkled. He was still as sharp as a tack.

"Ten years in the slammer, son. You earned your wings. I'll get my ol' lady to put 'em on your cut. An' get Crow to add 'em to your tats."

Zak nodded to avoid creating any drama, but he didn't want the wings. On his cut, on his body, or otherwise. He wasn't proud of being a convict. A felon.

A jailbird.

And he didn't need a permanent reminder of that, either. But he kept that to himself.

"Okay, enough of this fuckin' mushy homecoming. It's time to party like real men. Bonfire's rollin', pig's turnin', and there's plenty of pussy for everyone."

Zak turned toward the bar and saw Pierce, the current club president, standing on the polished surface, high above everyone crowded around it. A collective shout went up at his announcement and the crowd started filing out the side door to the courtyard where they had an outdoor pavilion, picnic tables, and all the shit they needed to party like a club should.

More people patted him on the back as they passed him. Some he knew. Some he didn't. Some wore cuts, and a few of the women wore them, too.

Ol' ladies.

He wondered how many of the members were now saddled with a ball and chain.

Fresh out of the box, he was going to make sure he didn't have any of the female hang-arounds dig her claws into him. When it was warm enough to drag his bike out, he wanted no one on the back clinging on to him. He had plenty of time for that later.

Now... Now, he was going to enjoy life.

But first, he was going to get shit-faced. Then get laid. Or vice versa.

Zak hooted loudly, then got swept outside with the rest of the crowd.

Get it here:
Down & Dirty: Zak (Dirty Angels MC, Book 1)

IF YOU ENJOYED THIS BOOK

Thank you for reading DAMAGED. If you enjoyed it, please consider leaving a review at your favorite retailer and/or Goodreads to let other readers know. Reviews are always appreciated and just a few words can help an independent author like me tremendously!

Want to read a sample of her work? Download a sampler book here: BookHip.com/MTQQKK

ALSO BY JEANNE ST. JAMES

* Available in Audiobook

Made Maleen: A Modern Twist on a Fairy Tale *

Damaged *

Rip Cord: The Complete Trilogy *

Brothers in Blue Series:

(Can be read as standalones)

Brothers in Blue: Max *

Brothers in Blue: Marc *

Brothers in Blue: Matt *

Teddy: A Brothers in Blue Novelette *

Brothers in Blue: A Bryson Family Christmas *

The Dare Ménage Series:

(Can be read as standalones)

Double Dare *

Daring Proposal *

Dare to Be Three *

A Daring Desire *

Dare to Surrender *

A Daring Journey *

The Obsessed Novellas:

(All the novellas in this series are standalones)

Forever Him *

Only Him *

Needing Him *

Loving Her *

Tempting Him *

Down & Dirty: Dirty Angels MC Series®:

Down & Dirty: Zak *

Down & Dirty: Jag *

Down & Dirty: Hawk *

Down & Dirty: Diesel *

Down & Dirty: Axel *

Down & Dirty: Slade *

Down & Dirty: Dawg *

Down & Dirty: Dex *

Down & Dirty: Linc *

Down & Dirty: Crow *

Crossing the Line (A DAMC/Blue Avengers Crossover) *

Magnum: A Dark Knights MC/Dirty Angels MC Crossover *

Crash: A Dirty Angels MC/Blood Fury MC Crossover

Guts & Glory Series:

(In the Shadows Security)

Guts & Glory: Mercy *

Guts & Glory: Ryder *

Guts & Glory: Hunter *

Guts & Glory: Walker *

Guts & Glory: Steel *

Guts & Glory: Brick *

Blood & Bones: Blood Fury MC®:

Blood & Bones: Trip *

Blood & Bones: Sig *

Blood & Bones: Judge *

Blood & Bones: Deacon *

Blood & Bones: Cage *

Blood & Bones: Shade

Blood & Bones: Rook

Blood & Bones: Rev

Blood & Bones: Ozzy

Blood & Bones: Dodge

Blood & Bones: Whip

Blood & Bones: Easy

COMING SOON!

Everything About You (A Second Chance Gay Romance)

Double D Ranch (An MMF Ménage Series)

Blue Avengers MC™

ABOUT THE AUTHOR

JEANNE ST. JAMES is a USA Today and international bestselling romance author who loves writing about strong women and alpha males. She was only thirteen when she first started writing. Her first published piece was an erotic short story in Playgirl magazine. She then went on to publish her first romance novel in 2009. She is now an author of over fifty-seven contemporary romances. Along with writing M/F, M/M, and M/M/F ménages, she also writes under the name J.J. Masters.

To keep up with her busy release schedule check her website at www.jeannestjames.com or sign up for her newsletter: http://www.jeannestjames.com/newslettersignup

www.jeannestjames.com
jeanne@jeannestjames.com

Newsletter: http://www.jeannestjames.com/newslettersignup
Jeanne's FB Readers Group: https://www.facebook.com/groups/JeannesReviewCrew/
TikTok: https://www.tiktok.com/@jeannestjames
Audible: https://www.audible.com/author/Jeanne-St-James/B002YBDE7O

facebook.com/JeanneStJamesAuthor

twitter.com/JeanneStJames

amazon.com/author/jeannestjames

instagram.com/JeanneStJames

bookbub.com/authors/jeanne-st-james

goodreads.com/JeanneStJames

pinterest.com/JeanneStJames

Printed in Great Britain
by Amazon

83027962R00120